THE
TIGRESS
RETURNS

Sequel to the International seller Bollywood Beds & Beyond

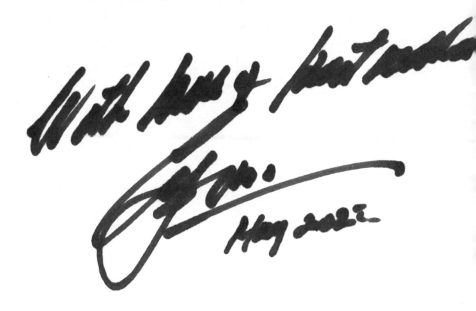

THE
TIGRESS
RETURNS

Sequel to the International seller Bollywood Beds & Beyond

CYRUS BHARUCHA

Notion Press

Old No. 38, New No. 6

McNichols Road, Chetpet

Chennai - 600 031

First Published by Notion Press 2016

Copyright © Cyrus Bharucha 2016

All Rights Reserved.

ISBN 978-93-5206-857-9

THE AUTHOR'S NOTES

This is a work of fiction and resemblance to anyone alive or dead is a coincidence. Some of the stories and 'information' in dialogues and narrative dealing with the war in Afghanistan and other stories have been taken from public domain spaces on the Internet.

Also like to thank my friend Lorraine More for her help in editing the story.

DEDICATION

To all the people who at one time or
another have helped me in my life.

They know who they are and I am ever so grateful to them.

CONTENTS

1. The Woman   1
2. Back in the Fold   5
3. You Must Be Joking!   13
4. Surprise   18
5. Return to the Past   25
6. 'Anita' Takes Over   28
7. Tito   38
8. The Attack   43
9. The New Life   52
10. The Meeting   57
11. Tito Returns   64
12. How What   70
13. Return to Base   73
14. A Tigress Never Loses Her Stripes   78
15. The Reporter   89
16. Beyond the R&R   93
17. In to the Unknown   97
18. The Bartered Bride   103
19. Dangerous Liasons   109
20. Return Home   113
21. The Dorabjee Family   118
22. Lovers in Mumbai   122
23. The Wrangling   129
24. It Never Ends   136
25. The Circus is Over   140
26. The Tigress in London   144
27. She Must Return   146
28. Zurich   152
29. The Chase   156
30. The Escape   160
    Author   *165*

1
THE WOMAN

The woman who had just been raped was sitting on a rock crying, thinking about how to escape.

Years ago she came to these parts as a dupe for the CIA and the New Jersey Police Department, aka NJPD, to foil a notorious murderer and arms dealer who had supplied weapons to the Taliban for years and to the Muslim rebels, the Lashkar Taiba or LeT one of the largest and most active Islamist terrorist organizations in South Asia operating mainly from Pakistan.

In the operation that went partly wrong the notorious Salim was released by the Taliban but later caught at the entrance of the Khyber Pass by the Pakistan forces and handed over to the USA. The woman who was sitting on the rock was captured and taken by the Taliban leader, who stripped her of her dignity and loveliness and raped her daily for months as they looked upon her as a common foreign whore.

She didn't even know what day it was or even the month. The years had taken a toll on her looks. The café au lait smooth skin was now dark coffee; her square jaw was lined on both cheeks and the bags under the eyes could carry a day's shopping. Those mango shaped breasts hung like udders and the legs were scarred and thicker. She hadn't had the nerve to look at herself in the mirror for ages.

The day was actually the first Tuesday in November 2004 and the world was anxiously awaiting the result of the US elections between President George. W. Bush and Senator John Kerry. A bitter election mainly over the war in Iraq that Bush had started over a year ago and the war in Afghanistan that was going on forever with Coalition and American forces being deployed. The election results came out that Bush had won and the wars would still continue.

Shilpa More (Moray), now 41 years old, sat on the rock and all she was aware of was the war in Afghanistan was still going on and the tribe she was with was hiding people from Al Qaeda and even Osama bin Laden at one point. He had offered to take Shilpa as his bride in exchange for six of his men and some firearms but the blue-eyed Taliban leader refused saying "She is not worthy of you and your family. Too many men have been there if you get my meaning."

How on earth am I going to get away from here? She thought, in fact that's all she ever thought about but not knowing the geography of this wild land she had no idea where in the world she was and this from a girl who knew the high life in Bombay (now Mumbai), London, New York and the European cities. What ever happened to the film star Ashok Kapoor, her father Ajit More the TV tycoon and that bloody Darius Cooper who she wished she hadn't treated so shabbily? Where are they now and I must be a dim blip, if at all, on their radar. She had been in Afghanistan since 1998.

That evening the NATO bombers came over and hammered the caves. Every other day they came and someone always died. Today it was a child and her father who was a fighter. The tribe buried the two under rocks, as the ground was too hard to dig and packed their belongings and started to move at dawn.

Three decades of war made Afghanistan one of the world's most dangerous countries. While the international community was rebuilding war-torn Afghanistan, terrorist groups such as the Haqqani Network and Islami were actively involved in a nationwide Taliban-led insurgency, which included hundreds of assassinations and suicide attacks.

The tribe she was associated with had sent in twelve-year-old boys and girls with bombs strapped to their bellies to ask the US soldiers for food and then they detonated themselves. The day after the tribe moved the leader looked through his binoculars and saw a platoon of soldiers in the distance.

He smiled and asked "Who wants to go to heaven today? Which of you boys want 72 virgins eh?"

"Me, Me, Me…" came a cry from the boys. The mothers started to cry and stop them but the leader convinced them this was for the glory of Allah and no glory is greater. Shilpa said she wanted to do the same, which horrified the tribe and the leader. After all she was no longer the beauty she was six years ago and had become an obedient wife and woman to all the men. Only one idiot had had his way with her the night before.

The leader went up to her and asked "Why do you do this for us? Do you believe in the supreme power?"

"Yes I do and I think God will forgive me for my sins if I do this now."

She thought of the famous lines of Sidney Carlton in a *Tale of Two Cites* and said aloud in Pashto "It is a far, far better thing I do now than I have ever done," with tears in her eyes she asked for the bomb belt, which was strapped around her and two of the boys.

The mothers hugged the boys, the fathers held them by their arms and thanked them for their sacrifice but no one said a word to Shilpa not even the leader who thought this is poetic justice for her life.

The platoon was a mile or so away so the three bombers started to walk with Shilpa in the middle holding the hands of the two boys. As they grew closer she could feel the sweat on the palms of the boys and one of them started to shake.

"Don't worry but do exactly as I say and you will not get hurt or feel anything. It will all be over very fast. Am I clear?

"Yes aunty," said the boys now shaking even more.

Shilpa looked back but couldn't see the tribe as they were over the curve of the barren, rocky terrain.

"Hello boys! Hello soldier boys!" she yelled.

Guns at the ready they turned to face the three hungry faces. "Please do not shoot! We are friends," she said in English, which was rarely heard in these parts.

"Stop! Who are you? ID yourself now and get on the ground-Now!" yelled the sergeant. They had their guns in firing positions as they approached the trio.

"Boys slowly undo your belts but don't make a quick move," Shilpa whispered.

"But why? Let them come twenty more feet and I will kill them," said the younger boy.

"Listen to me! I have a better idea to get all of them this way we will kill only two or three," said Shilpa.

The soldiers were British and walked very slowly towards the trio. "Put your arms in the air and do not move a muscle. Do you understand woman?" said a soldier.

"Yes we do. We have bombs on us..." yelled Shilpa.

The group of soldiers came to a sudden halt. "Are you serious?"

"Yes very, all three of us but we are not going to explode them. Hold the boys hands so they can't get to the trigger and mine too. I have asked them to undo the belts but not sure if they have. Be careful."

The boys looked up and were confused as to what was going on. Shilpa told them again to hold out their arms high, which they did and as the soldiers came near they lifted up coats of each one of them and saw the bomb belts under the flimsy goatskins.

"Hey Serge, this one is shaking so much the bloody things could go off by itself. Take it easy son, you are going to be OK," said the young private.

The squad separated them and walked them away from each other. The young boy was shaking and shivering a lot now in the cold November air and then BANG! The bomb went off and the boy and soldier were killed at once.

"Oh Jesus!" Cried out the captain who had been in the background the whole time. The squad turned their weapons on both Shilpa and the other boy. The boy called out, his whole body shaking and pointed to the belt on the ground behind him. Shilpa also called out and said her belt was "Off" but she could drop it if they wanted to undo it from the back. She kept her hands high as another private undid the belt and it fell to the ground.

The duo was then marched to the tent while others including the medic were trying to put together the body parts.

"Who the hell are you?" shouted the captain at Shilpa.

"Do you want the short or long version captain? But before we start or I start I need a good meal and some good coffee, same for the boy then we talk. OK?"

The private first gave her and the boy a small mug of brandy, which the kid drank as if it was his last drink, in two big gulps, and then burped and cried.

Back at the tribe they heard the bomb go off and thought it must have all gone well. But just one explosion that was odd thought the leader.

2
BACK IN THE FOLD

The private entered the tent with some beef sausages, fried eggs and a hot mug of tea for Shilpa and the boy who had now identified himself as Abdul Kareem, meaning servant of the generous creator, who it turned out was twelve years old just four days ago. The friend who died was only eleven.

"What a bloody waste of life," said Captain Ian Meade a graduate of Sandhurst.

"Bet she was a looker in her days sir," said Sergeant Collins a fifteen-year vet from Croydon, south of London.

"Yea you can see that can't you sergeant? Well let's listen to her story because she certainly isn't from around here," replied Meade.

"For starters lady lets have your full name and don't jerk us around OK or you'll be back where you just came from," said Collins.

"My name is Shilpa Moray spelt MORE. I am from India and was brought here many years ago. What month is it today?"

"Its November 2004…"

"Oh my God, I have been here for six years. I can't believe it," she closed her eyes and tears streamed down her face.

"Well I guess I have to start at the top captain. I hope you have a lot of time because it's going to be a long tale and one you may not believe," said Shilpa.

"Try me," said the captain.

"It all began years ago now. I was the daughter of a rich and powerful TV mogul in India and at the time, I now realise a pretty spoilt Bombay society lady. Never married, didn't need a man to support me as Daddy was there and never really fell in love. Could have at one time with Darius…" she went quiet and began to wander in her mind.

"Please pick up from days in Bombay," said the sergeant.

"Oh yes Bombay, I so miss it now. Well I was involved in bidding for a TV station in the USA, an Indian station that an actor called Ashok Kapoor and some other people were after it as well. The actor, a big star in India and my father were hankering for it as a money laundering operation, whereas the others were using it as a front to deal in arms with the Taliban here. It's all very complicated. You really want to hear all this?" Shilpa asked.

Both the men nodded but first told the corporal to take the boy Abdul to a tent and let him sleep. They would talk to him in the morning.

"I had long wanted to be free of my parents and so when they gave me my inheritance early I wanted to have my own TV station and business. So I went after this one in New York."

What she was carefully avoiding was telling them of the number of people she slept with in order to try and secure this station including the film star, the man she called Darius with whom she played dastardly tricks, Alan the financier who she made sure died by sending him a whore who knowingly had AIDS, the owner of the station who was later shot, one Jerry Patel, well she never really had sex with him but drugged him so he thought he had sex with her and finally one of the ringleaders Salim, the slime, who brought her to Afghanistan. But then the rest of the story was sort of true with a number of gaps.

"I was at a meeting with the owner Jerry Patel and his partners in America. One of the partners was Salim, who brought me here, but when he realised that Jerry was double crossing him and the other partners he shot him and that is how the New Jersey Police came into the picture. This led to the discovery of the fact that the TV station was a front for this Indian Mafia and they were making money-shipping arms via the Gulf States to Pakistan and then to Afghanistan and Pakistan held Kashmir. I got caught up in it thanks to the shooting of Jerry," she paused and thought for a minute.

"I was put in prison in India but the New Jersey Police and CIA made a deal with me if I was to help them catch Salim, the main man in this operation, that would lead them to the others in the Gulf and Pakistan. I offered to go under the care of the CIA but they lost me in the Khyber Pass. My GPS went out of range and the Taliban took me prisoner after they took the arms from Salim. I have never known what ever happened to him and the others I knew. The leader of the tribe that took the arms made me his wife so to speak. My skin crawls at the thought of it. Here I am six years later. I saw this operation of blowing you guys up as a chance to escape," sighed Shilpa and dropped her head on the table.

"Well I think that will do for tonight, we'll pick it up in the morning," said Captain Meade.

Shilpa was got up slowly and lay down on an air mattress where she slept for the next six hours.

The following morning the platoon set off for their base in Helmand. The UK forces were fighting under the name of Operation Herrick where they were being supported by the local Afghan forces that were helping to keep the Taliban out.

At the base the boy was taken into custody while Shilpa was taken to an interrogation room where she was asked about her dealings with the Taliban tribe, where they hide and who was with them, where did they get their arms and who was supplying them. The interview went on for 4 hours at the end of which the old spark came back to Shilpa and she demanded a bath, some good food, especially ice cream, new clothes and a bed to sleep only then would she talk. After six years of what she called a living hell she wanted just the basics of a civil life. She got everything she wanted.

She stood in the hot shower for over fifteen minutes till a woman corporal called out to her to get a move on. "Come on luv, this isn't the Dorchester you know. Water is very precious here."

When Shilpa walked out into the camp hut for women soldiers, a mirror confronted her, for the first time in ages where she saw the body men so desired now looking haggard and unfit. It made her cry. She sat on a bunk bed wrapped in a towel and just cried her eyes out. The corporal watched her and decided to leave her alone in the dorm. She was finally free.

Over the next few days the interviews continued where she was told the boy Abdul Kareem had been sent to an orphanage in Kandahar. The Army was keen to find the tribe and catch the leader. They needed Shilpa's help in identifying him so it meant she was to stay on the base and wear an army uniform of a sergeant so as not to be conspicuous.

Four days after she had been at the base the commander told her that she was to go out with Captain Meade and his platoon leaders to find the tribe and bring back the chief and the fighters if they could, if not kill him and the others on the spot.

In the British Army, a rifle platoon from an infantry company consists of three sections of eight men, plus a signaler (radio operator), a platoon sergeant, the platoon commander (either a second lieutenant or lieutenant) and a mortar man operating a light mortar (full strength of 27 men and one officer).

Each section is commanded by a corporal, with a lance corporal as second-in-command and six privates divided into two four-man fire teams. Other types of platoons (such as mortar or anti-tank platoons) are generally smaller and are commanded by a lieutenant or captain. An armored "platoon" is known as a "Troop."

They travelled north into the mountains, that jutted out like great slabs of iron which were slashed with white snow, but Shilpa was honest to say she had no idea as to where they went as it was not something she was ever concerned about but she knew some land marks. One of them was a public garden that must have been beautiful in its day with fruit orchards all around but now in disarray.

The army had a spot like that on the map so they moved towards it. It was also an area the planes didn't bomb so it was possible the tribe had moved there now but normally it was their summer retreat. A day and a half later they reached the garden and the park where some old people were walking. The Afghan translator went up to them and asked if there were new people in the town but there was no answer from the old folks.

Meade then told Shilpa to go to them and offer them food and some cold drinks they had brought to bribe the locals- chocolates, biscuits, nuts and bottles of black currant juice. The old folks tore open the wrappers and consumed the food as if they hadn't eaten for days. In fact they hadn't seen this sort of food in years.

"Two days ago a tribe of people came and are staying at the north side of the town. They are Taliban, we think so, because they come usually only in summer and do not mix with us," said an old man who was relishing the Cadbury chocolate.

Thirty minutes later the platoon was on the outskirts of the northern part of the town. The sun was beginning to set and the temperature had dropped to five Celsius. A queue of women dressed in black burkas and carrying tin cans of water came out of the houses and walked to the trees.

"Blimey Serge what them women up to then?" asked a Cockney Private.

"They are going to do their potty you might say. It's sunset and it gives the women privacy to do their thing now and the men all stay inside to respect them."

"Well its all the bloody respect they ever get from those dozy bastards," replied the private.

"Quiet! No more talking we move in three minutes from now. Check watches 18.35 move at 18.38. Lieutenant Ambrose will take the right side door and Catlow will take the rear, I will charge in the front with Sergeant Collins covering me. Roger and Out," said Captain Meade over the radio.

Shilpa's mind suddenly went back to Ashok Kapoor and his films and thought he would have loved this but it was for real and people were going to die in a few minutes, a shiver went up her spine.

The Platoon very slowly approached the building where no one stirred and then with a sudden force Meade had a private break down the door and rushed in to find the Taliban men ready for them and the burst of fire came from both sides.

The first private who opened the door was hit in the shoulder and Lt. Catlow was hit in the thigh, a corporal was shot straight through the head, destroying his helmet. On the other hand five Taliban lay dead and the leader was injured in the arm and the lower leg so couldn't move. Screaming of the women could be heard outside as Sergeant Collins tried to calm them down. It was all over for the moment and the children came out of the houses where they had been hiding asking for chocolate as if nothing had happened.

The first thing was to see to the injured by two medics after which Meade asked for Shilpa to identify the women. Their jaws dropped when they saw "their Shilpa" dressed in army uniform and wearing sun glasses to protect her eyes from shrapnel.

"What happened to my son?" asked one of the women. Shilpa just shook her head and the woman began to scream and cry–'the wailing and gnashing of teeth had begun.'

"What about my Abdul?" yelled another woman.

"He is fine, Abdul is in a good home now run by the Americans. He will go to school and have a wonderful life in time," said Shilpa feeling sorry for the mothers but also remembered what a horrendous life she had with them for six years. On the whole the women had been kind to her not like those bloody men.

"You recognized him?" asked the Captain pointing to a man in handcuffs and two soldiers holding their gun barrels against his body

"Yes that's him. Amjal Khan." She went to him looked him square in the eye and spat on his face and then hit him in the crotch. He doubled over but didn't make a sound even though a bullet had scraped his leg.

"Stop! We are not going to do this as much as I know you want to. He will be tried and hopefully put away for the rest of his life," said Meade.

"I want to see him hung, drawn and quartered. You have no idea what he and his men have done to me in the past six years. I can never have a child thanks to these bastards," she swung her right hand and punched him in the jaw.

"Enough now take her away. And you (talking to Amjal) try to get away and I will shoot you where she first hit you. Put four guards on him and keep the other two separated. One in each Range Rover," said the captain. There were three RRs and four armoured cars. Shilpa rode with the captain in the front car away from the Taliban.

Back at the base the three Taliban men were put in high security lockups with no food or water for a day to soften them up for interrogation. The cells were bleak, cream coloured, a metal bed and pot to piss in but no sheets or washbasin. Over the next three days the men were interviewed separately and often beaten if the right answer wasn't forthcoming.

Amjal Khan wouldn't say a word but the others finally talked under pressure. The medical unit took a blood test and tried to do a DNA match but all they could come up with was he was not Afghan but mid-European Muslim or convert. Even the water torture and sleep deprivation they put him through didn't make him talk. It was like he had taken a vow of silence. Finally it was time to send them to Kabul where the Afghans would deal with them and that would make water torture seem like a baby's bath.

After Shilpa had been there for ten days the army offered to take her to Kabul and stay in a hotel and buy some women's clothes. She took the offer and as soon as she entered the room of the best hotel in Afghanistan she rushed to the bathroom and ran a bath where she soaked for over an hour till the water ran cold. After that she got into bed in the nude and slept for over ten hours with a 'Do Not Disturb' notice on the door.

The next morning when she went down for breakfast she was shocked to find a press gallery at the entrance of the lift. Flash bulbs went off and questions started to flow from the crowd.

"Shilpa where were you for all these years? Who have you been with? Did the Taliban torture you? Were you raped?" she was so shocked she jumped back in the elevator and went to her room and ordered breakfast.

At 8.30 am the phone rang, it was the British Embassy's PR woman apologizing for the leak to the press and telling her to stay indoors till she arrived. Within thirty minutes Jill Adams came to the door. Seeing this immaculate blond lady in heels and a grey pant suit, her head lightly covered by a pale grey Pashmina shawl, Shilpa felt like a cat who had been dragged out of the gutter.

"Hello, I'm Jill Adams from the embassy. Let's talk inside," she said at the door.

The two women sat and Shilpa again went into her story this time telling Jill about her stay in the Indian prison and how the CIA rescued her from prison by setting up a phony police force and took her to a charter flight out of Bombay to New Jersey where they asked her to take part in the project to bring in Salim and drop the charges against her if she was willing to be a tool in the scheme.

She found it easier to talk to Jill and the two women even laughed at the story of her going to Puerto Rico with Jerry Patel and how he drooled over her naked body till the Ambien kicked in and he fell asleep. When he woke up Shilpa told him he was such a tiger in bed that she was going to be sore for the next three days and that kept Jerry happy so he simply played with himself looking at her laying nude on the bed. But as for Salim he was a brute, the bastard, those memories came flooding back. Jill was amazed at her frankness and then said they needed to get all this on video in the next few days. The thought of being photographed upset Shilpa seeing the way she now looked.

"I want to go home. When can I go home?" Shilpa asked the chief PRO at the embassy.

"Well we have a problem luv, you see, we the British, found you but you are an Indian national and if we let you go now they will claim you and right now you still have charges pending against you in India. The statues of limitations run for seven years and you have been away for only six so you could be in trouble there. We think you should be sent to England ASAP."

"What am I going to do in London? I don't know anyone there now and won't the Indian government ask for me to be deported?"

"Well anything is possible but we want you to be our source for the internal side of the Taliban. You are educated, you've lived with them and know them very intimately one can say, right?"

"I hope this is not a case from the frying pan into the fire!"

Over the next few days Jill took Shilpa out of the hotel on a tour of Kabul. It wasn't exactly a tourist destination but it beat being indoors and they sampled some good local food not the rubbish she had consumed for six years.

More than a week past in Kabul with interviews and side trips to the city, then one evening Jill came to see Shilpa and told her to pack as she was going to London that night. The two women packed her stuff into one case and a handbag and took the back elevator to a car waiting for them straight to the airport.

The plane was a Hercules C130K, the workhorse of the RAF, its large cave like interior has transported tanks to VIPs all over the world. Shilpa had never been in anything like this and she just stood in awe and said, "Good God, does this really take off?"

The flight to London took 12 hours and landed at a secret airstrip with very few buildings and even fewer lights. The tower guided the plane onto the runway and then to a complete halt where two Land Rovers came up to the rear doors where Shilpa and Jill were escorted to the cars and then within minutes they were on the motorway towards London. The escort-service had coffee and sandwiches for the passengers but no loo stops for almost three hours. Even Jill had no idea where they had landed but then the signs showed up on the M1 which told them they had landed somewhere near Birmingham. The cars drove up to the "hotel" in Drayton Gardens, a small flat but secure which the MI6 used as a safe house.

"Welcome to your new home Ms. More (as in- 'more') make yourself comfortable and we will get you almost anything you want as far as food, books, DVDs and allow you a few calls in the presence of an officer. Otherwise you stay quiet and please don't roam around London, as you will have a tail. Hope that is crystal clear?" said a man looking very much like a World War 2 RAF officer with a large moustache and a double -breasted blazer.

It was now after 4 pm and Shilpa asked where the tea was and offered to make it for all three officers and Jill. They were amused and accepted the offer; she even found a Harrods fruit cake and biscuits in the larder.

"I still can't believe this is happening to me," she said. "Years ago I was kidnapped from an Indian jail and brought to America and now almost the same way to London. How long am I going to be here and then what?"

"Mam you are here at Her Majesty's pleasure and so that could mean a long time. It's not a free deal so to speak but tomorrow when you come to the office we will fill you in. As for now enjoy the tea, Charlie here will bring you some Chinese food and join you for the night and then in the morning another officer will accompany you to the office – The SIS – Secret Intelligent Service often called MI6. James Bond and all that rubbish," he smiled as he said that and twirled his handlebar moustache.

That night Shilpa didn't sleep well she woke up Charlie in the living room a couple of times to chat but saw Charlie was in no mood to listen so she went back to bed and waited for the morning.

3
YOU MUST BE JOKING!

The SIS or MI6 (Military Intelligence section 6) building in London stands at Vauxhall Cross on the south bank of the river Thames. The MI6 has had a chequered history since its inception in the early part of the 20th century. It played an important part in WW1 and then during the second war it was overshadowed by other agencies like the code busters of Bletchley Park, the "Imaginary Activity" run by the RAF and the "double cross" by the MI5 to feed misleading intelligence to the Germans. John Le Carrie with his stories about the secret service and Ian Fleming with his James Bond novels revived its fame in the 1950s and 60s. Most people even today know the Secret Intelligent Service or SIS by its old name MI6.

People who work in it are called "spooks" made famous by the BBC TV series "Spooks." The terms used by people inside the SIS call it the "Office" and those outside it like the press calls it the "Firm." Earlier Shilpa was associated with the "Agency or Company" which was the CIA in the USA.

Shilpa arrived at Sir Terry Fennel's magnificent building that has been the home of the SIS since 1995. It's been made bomb-proof and featured in several Bond films as a place that cannot be destroyed. She was in awe, to say the least, of the place and still couldn't believe it was only a month since she escaped from the Taliban. Wearing a long black dress with a red jacket, picked out by Jill, she made herself presentable for the interview.

"Welcome to London Ms. Moray. May I suggest you change the spelling of your name so we idiot Brits can get it right in our strange spelling language. It would be so much easier for us to say it correctly if spelt MORAY, don't you think?" said the division Director who was not introduced by name.

"I will think it over for sure. You may be right now I have a new life in England," said Shilpa feeling very confident again.

Over the next few hours and lunch Shilpa told them her story this time bringing in the opium deals that Amjal Khan made with anyone who was ready to pay in dollars. They used the money to get arms from dealers in Iran and Uzbekistan and even the Chinese. He seldom gave the tribe any money except to buy simple food and occasionally clothes in the winter months.

She then shocked the SIS man and his team by telling them opium was also sold to the CIA and the MI6.

"I think your people and the CIA are in Afghanistan to help manage the one hundred billion dollar a year drug industry, moving heroin through Afghanistan, managing the banking for the heroin industry through London banks. I can't think of anything else they would do there."

"You must be joking lady," said an intelligence officer sitting at the end of the table. The others stayed very quiet.

"There is no reason for the US or Britain to be in Afghanistan other than the fact that they do not seem to have the common sense to leave after the battle with the Taliban who they licked and now have to battle the likes of my tribe," said Shilpa.

This was the last thing they wanted to hear.

"Amjal said that they have always managed the world's opium and heroin trafficking. It is something the British Empire is known for. The British began heroin certainly opium production in Afghanistan. They have been doing it for well over a hundred years and it is extremely profitable. It funds all of their other activities and there is no reason for them to want to leave it. You people do not have the capability to impact the intelligence or military situation in Afghanistan in a positive way, whatsoever. You lot and the Americans are clueless. The CIA put trackers in my shoes, my purse and in my bra and the bastards lost me and handed me over to the bloody Taliban to be raped and degraded for years. What the hell do you want with me?" Shilpa raised her voice for the first time since escaping and the frustration now poured out.

"You never said all this before," said Jill, it was now clear she was a SIS agent planted in the embassy. 'Why didn't you tell me this before?" she asked.

"You never asked me did you?"

"This is very sensitive stuff we are discussing here Ms. Moray. You can't talk about this to anyone outside this room," said the Director. "You know far more than we imagined or even thought a woman from Afghanistan would know—goodness me!" Said the Director.

"So what were you expecting an ugly bimbo? I have been through a lot that none of you in this room can even begin to imagine and I have a lot of info on these bastards but before we go any further I want a deal. Please do not insult me by saying Her Majesty's government doesn't make deals, you do it all the time and it's time for one now gentlemen and lady," she said smiling at Jill.

The Director left the room with his aide who then returned to join the others and said a deal could be reached within reason.

Shilpa laid out her first set of terms: Money in the bank in her name. 30,000 Pounds, a face and body lift, which brought a smile to everyone's face including her's, a flat away from the safe house, two bedrooms and two baths. A small rented car and a credit card that she could use in an emergency, which the service would pay for but only for a year and finally no deportation to India – ever.

"Fine" the Director agreed but in turn she was to be a member of the SIS and paid 50 Pounds a week for her services on top of the deal just struck. She would be called for at any time of day and had to perform for the country, which was now her new home.

"Agreed," said Shilpa and they all shook on it and the paperwork was set into motion. "You know Shilpa I never thought you had it in you when we met a month ago," said Jill. "You have a terrific deal and so if I may say so don't push it too much now, at least for the time being," said Jill tapping her on the shoulders.

Within a week Shilpa was moved to St. Mary's Terrace in Little Venice off the Edgware Rd. in London. Large Victorian flats were made for middle class families over 100 years ago now they were homes to the trendy upper middle class. She loved to walk around the canal along Warwick Avenue and down to Paddington station where there was so much life. The main Edgware road was now an Arab street where the Gulf States had moved in during the 1980s. It was full of cafes and restaurants catering only to the Arab taste and students who wanted to be different and smoke hookahs.

Once the flat was fixed she was taken to a Harley Street clinic for her nip and tuck as she called it. In fact there were three operations over three weeks. First the face, then the breasts and finally the stomach and lipo-suction on the buttocks. After several hours in the gym and three months later Shilpa was a new woman. No one from the past would know her now and some said she looked like Elizabeth Taylor in her prime. If only my friends could see me now, she thought.

There was something missing in Shilpa's life and that was a man. She had been tempted to call an escort agency but then she knew there was always a tail on her; some poor slobs had a really boring job trailing her. One night she saw this spook outside the building and it was cold. He was in and out of the car to keep himself warm and from getting bored.

"Want to come up for a coffee?" called out Shilpa.

"Can I come up and bring it down?"

"Oh just come up and get warm, must be boring down there."

He was up to the second floor in less than a minute and the door was open so he walked it. He was not very tall about 5'-8" and well built. She suddenly thought of Darius who hadn't entered her mind in weeks.

"Hi, what's your name or can't I ask?" she smiled and held out a mug of fresh coffee.

"Oh you can call me Ray. You know how it is with us," said the handsome dark haired man. He didn't look English so in time it came out he was born in Brazil to an English mother and Brazilian father. Ray came to the UK when he was five after the parents divorced and he grew up here. Didn't have much to do so tried to be a pro footballer but wasn't good enough so joined the service as a driver and then worked his way up to his present position.

He sat on the couch and drank his coffee but not relaxed at all. Shilpa walked over to him and ran her hand through his hair, which was black and thick. "Please mam don't do that. I should go down. Thanks for the coffee," said Ray and got up to leave.

Shilpa walked up to him and without saying a word took his face in her hands and kissed him on the lips gently and then again with more passion and before long they were on the sofa with her kimono around her waist, his shirt off and her hands pulling down his zipper.

When she touched his groin she squealed with delight and he ravaged her breasts like he hadn't had sex for years. She couldn't remember when she last felt like this. They moved in unison so well that Shilpa screamed, "Oh God that was amazing!" She couldn't stop taking in gasps of air and he slumped to the floor with his trousers still around his ankles and his shirt open.

Ray felt dizzy and hoped to God there wasn't a CCTV camera in the flat.

"Mam, do you know if the flat has surveillance cameras?"

"I think after this episode you can call me Shilpa or even "luv" like you English like to say," said naked Shilpa her legs wide open on the sofa. "God knows, I am sure knowing your lot there are somewhere. Sorry I didn't mean to get you into trouble."

The folks back at the HQ saw a really good "XXX show" that night. Sadly they had to report it in the morning.

"What the bloody hell does Romano think he is doing?" yelled the Director.

"Bonking Shilpa by the looks of it sir," said the aide. "She is better than most of the pornos I have seen. Now there's a career for her sir. Get her bonking the Taliban and get their secrets"

"Don't be an ass Jim I think she's had enough of those bastards and they made a mess of her. Poor kid but she is smart and now is the time to put her to work. Get her in here will you, let's talk to the bored lady and give her something to get her teeth into. And tell that Mexican or whatever he is to keep his zipper done up or next time he is fired," said the Director.

After lunch Shilpa entered the Director's office looking very glamorous straight out of a Bond movie. "Well you do look good Ms. Moray I have to say. I have a daughter your age and I must say she doesn't hold a patch to you. Anyway she has taken after me, all brains and no looks," he laughed and Shilpa made an effort to smile.

"I have a job for your skills Shilpa and it's going to take you out of the country to Iraq. I want you to go there and get to know the top brass in the army those who are really loyal to us and those who still support Saddam Hussein. We will give you the intros but how you get them to talk is up to you if you know what I mean," smiled the Director.

"Are you serious? You must be joking," she said. The Director shook his head and she knew it was final. Shilpa returned to the flat and packed a bag ready to leave in a couple of days.

4
SURPRISE

The flight was from Northolt airport in north London. A charter from JAL was to take Shilpa and several others to Iraq and there they would split up to do their assigned duties. Forty-seven people were on the flight but very few knew each other. No one knew Shilpa. She was given a seat on her own in what would have been the first class in a normal flight.

Seven hours into the flight Shilpa asked the steward when they would land and was told in a couple of hours. "Why, has the pilot taken a long route to Baghdad?"

The steward just shrugged his shoulders and walked away.

After ten hours they landed and when the doors opened and Shilpa walked out she yelled "You fucking bastards! You conned me! You are no better than them!"

She had landed in Kabul.

As the passengers passed her sitting on the aircraft steps no one bothered to even ask her why she was upset they just behaved as if nothing had happened. How very English she thought. She recalled a time when her art student friends in London stripped off and painted their bodies with road signs and stood in the middle of Oxford Street and hardly any one stopped to look at them. One little boy did and his mother told him it was rude to stare and walked on.

A major from the battalion came over and introduced himself and told Shilpa he was her liaison while in Afghanistan.

"It's my job to make sure you meet the right people and do whatever it is you have to do. They were very hush-hush about you mam so I presume you are a VIP in these circles and so I have to take care of you."

"Thank you major I didn't get your name," said Shilpa softly and in shock.

"Julian Summers mam. Attached to Intel and all that."

"Young to be a major aren't you?"

"Well if you think 31 is young then I am but there are a few of us in this rank and one of my batch is a half colonel. Promotion is fast in combat zones. My dad was a full colonel in Korea when he was just 35."

Enough of rank talk thought Shilpa, nice looking kid though.

"Tomorrow night is a party to which we are invited and you will meet everyone from President Karzai to the local commanders. It's a big deal for the locals as we will be catering and the food has been flown in from London on your plane. Now let's get you to the hotel and you rest up," said the Major Summers.

When Shilpa enter the ballroom of the hotel, the following night, you would never think a war was raging twenty miles outside the city. No alcohol was in sight but there was a drinking room, which was only for the foreigners and for Afghan "friends," and there were many of them in the Pump room. The single malt whisky was flowing like water. Shilpa went in with Summers and helped herself to a scotch and water but to her surprise Summers only took a tomato juice. They then went out to mingle.

"General Aziz this is Anita Raj from Mumbai she is writing a book on the gardens of your country," said the major.

Anita Raj! He never warned me about this, what's going on?

Big smile "Hello, so nice to meet you general. What a fabulous country you have and it's going to be even better when this nasty little war is over, but I must say there is sand everywhere even in the bed," said Shilpa all giggles and smiles. The Major was impressed at the act.

They walked on and she tugged hard at his sleeve "What was that about, Anita Raj? Why the hell didn't you warn me you stupid man," she was angry.

"Sorry following orders. I think they wanted to see how you would react in a surprise situation and all I can say is you passed with flying colours. By the way from now on you are Anita Raj even your room is under that name. Open your purse please." She did and he placed something into it. "Look at it later no rush."

She was the belle of the ball. The President spent ten minutes talking to her about his childhood playing in the gardens near his home and he hoped that soon they would blossom again once the war was over. Generals and colonels came up to Shilpa to introduce themselves. After a while the major thought his job was redundant. Shilpa's handbag was filling up with cards and phone numbers. One older general came up and asked if she was related to Elizabeth Taylor in Hollywood because he swore they were like twins.

After Julian Summers had seen her back to her room he returned to his office and reported that the evening was a resounding success and she was simply brilliant especially the way she flirted with all the men. When she got back she opened her purse to find a mini phone-cam in it.

The next phase was to get her into a more intimate setting like a small dinner party but in the meantime Summers took her to see some ruins, which were once beautiful gardens just in case they were being watched. She was seen taking notes and photographs' of the battered bushes and trees.

That evening the Press attaché's wife swept into the room of her home where some of the guests had gathered and took Shilpa by the arm "Darling I must have you meet General Yusef Aziz who commands the local garrison."

"We met briefly last night Miss Raj. I can hardly forget you," said the general who was a tall man with a blackened moustache, grey at the temples and ruddy skin a mark of a man who has been weathered in the mountains.

They talked gardens, politics and TV programmes that Anita was going to make on her return trip.

"Ms. Raj from which country you are?" asked the general.

"London. Been living there for years,"

"Interesting because you don't speak like a Brit more like Indian but who is convent educated. Am I right?"

"You are good general. When were you in India?"

"Many years ago when the Russians were here and I was posted to my embassy in Delhi. I know India well and still have friends there," said the general letting her know he is checking her out. "What was the paper you are writing for?"

"I am not, I am doing a book and possibly a film of Now and Then sort of thing. It will take a few years as the gardens need to come back to their full glory so I will be coming back to take shots and write as the work progresses. Your President told me last night it's a priority so people can feel good and happy."

More small talk and they were seated next to each other at table when he touched her leg and pressed something against it. His hand went down to her lap and he slipped his card into her palm. Then looked at her and quietly said "I hope to see you soon, may be tomorrow and I will drive you to one of the few gardens still in reasonable shape." Shilpa accepted and so a date was made for 10 am next morning.

At exactly 10 am there was a knock on the door and a sergeant from the Afghan army stood at attention and gave Shilpa a note, which said to follow the man who had given her the note. They drove out of the city and then on a long bombed road she saw what must have been a paradise on earth. Roses still grew, lilies, tulips and poppies with green lawns separating the beds. At the far end was a gazebo with doors and curtains flowing in the breeze. The sergeant pointed to the Gazebo and told her to go and wait there for the general.

She pushed the curtains aside and inside was a setting out of a Hollywood film. The room had Rattan furniture with soft silk cushions, a magnificent

Persian carpet of red, gold and royal blue on the floor. A glass table made out of one piece of bent glass and on it were dishes of caviar from Iran, crackers, a variety of cheeses from Europe, nuts and fresh fruit and a bottle of Moet champagne on ice. She stood there not knowing what to do and was startled when a hand touched her shoulder. She turned around frightened to see who it was. The man held her head and planted a heavy kiss on her lips. She struggled and pushed him away only to see it was Yusef Aziz himself forcing himself on her.

"Was that the sort of welcome you expected?" he asked.

"No it bloody well wasn't and don't act like a pig with me" she stormed out of the gazebo.

He ran after her but seeing the soldier driver he stopped and called out "You have left this behind."

She turned and walked back to get her handbag as he went into the gazebo. When she entered he smiled and said, "I like a woman with sprit, you have it and I admire you. Can we start again please?"

Oh Lord I have a job to do so I better get on with it. "Don't you ever do that to me again. I am not a whore you pick up in London or Delhi."

He nodded but no apology. Shilpa was used to these men and their ways after all the only difference between this pig and the Taliban was the uniform.

They opened the champers and then started to laugh at a few jokes he had memorized for these situations. Some were raunchy which he had got off the Internet. Shilpa loved the caviar and allowed him to feed her one cracker at a time. Then came the grapes one at a time as she was stretched out on the chaise with the down-feathered cushions. His hand went behind the sofa and music came on softly playing Chopin's nocturnes. Oh God now I am the dessert she thought. Well not tonight Napoleon. She moved his hand away from her leg and sat up. "Don't be in such a hurry 'Mon generale,'" she said in a voice she hadn't used for years. "Play your cards right and then we will see but not today."

Aziz went into a sulk and she was happy to see it. Good, let the bastard sweat it out for a few days then I will take him for all he has.

The time passed and it was now after 2 pm so the general knowing he was batting on a bad wicket called it a day and drove Anita, as he knew her back to the hotel.

"See you tomorrow?" he asked.

"No but may be soon."

Trying to be charming he took her hand and kissed it, she smiled and got out of the 1980 Mercedes.

As soon as she entered the room the phone rang. It was the major asking how it went. She told him and he agreed with her to keep him waiting a few days in the meantime he wanted her to come to the office tomorrow for lunch to meet another general and tribal chief.

Spring in Afghanistan is a lovely time. It's warming up and some of the flowers are in bloom. Shilpa as Anita entered the home of Major Summers' who had invited a woman captain and the major general along with the tribal chief. When Anita saw the chief her heart stopped, she almost blurted out "Khalid" but stopped in time realising there was no way he would even think of putting her together with the Shilpa of old.

Once again the general, one Hamid Khan, made a date with Anita but this time she told him to call on her and not send a driver. It would be his honour at 8 pm tonight. As they were leaving Anita put out her hand to shake with the chief, he didn't take her hand but whispered "So you have forgotten your Afghan manners already in a few months," said the chief winking at Anita. "Yes Anita nice name for you now."

She looked at him trying to act as if she didn't know what was going on and just shook her head.

"You may have changed your face and name but not your voice. I remember voices very well and you don't hear voice like yours in these parts. The court in Kandahar hanged your husband Amjal Khan, did you know?"

She just stared back at him without saying a word and walked back to the host.

"Julian he knows" she said to the major.

"Knows what?"

"Who I am. He said he recognized my voice and told me of the other leader Amjal Khan my tribal chief had been hanged by the Afghan court. He knows for sure. Is he on our side?"

"I bloody well hope so. Jesus Christ! I need to get in touch with London."

"Listen Julian keep the carrot dangling but make sure the big stick is ready to be used, know what I mean?" said the Director in London on a secured line to Kabul.

"Anita may not be willing to dangle too much knowing what she knows now. I mean her life is in danger. So what is plan B sir?" asked Julian Summers.

"Haven't got one yet. Damn, didn't see this coming, our fault," sighed the Director.

At 8 pm sharp there was a knock on 'Anita's' door. Major General Hamid Khan stood there with a large bunch of red roses and dressed in civvies. "Hello gorgeous! You look even better in the evenings," he tried to kiss her cheek but she moved her head back discreetly saying she was ready to leave.

The 1975 Buick drove into an army compound and then to a bungalow, which had the general's name on it. Inside a table had been laid with whisky and wine bottles on a cart. "I hope you enjoy Afghan food. Have you ever had it?"

What Shilpa knew about real Afghan cooking wasn't worth writing about so she shook her head and then the general gave her a history lesson:

"The beauty of Afghan cuisine is its rich mixture of cultures, mainly influenced by that of Persia, Iran, India and Mongolia. From India came chillies, saffron, garam masala, cardamom, cinnamon, cloves, cumin, nutmeg and pepper. Persia contributed coriander, mint and cooking with spinach or green herbs. Then in the 13th century Genghis Khan brought Mongolian influences like dumplings and noodles. But Afghan cuisine has a style of its own. Fatty dishes are an important fuel in this nation of harsh landscapes and freezing winters. Afghans like their food neither too spicy nor too hot, and they are renowned for their use of dried fruit and nuts. They have a flair for rice, with yoghurt used as a dressing so you see my dear you are in for a treat as you Brits like to say."

Two soldier bearers served the food and then coffee was taken in the sitting room.

"You would like to participate in this?" He asked holding up a joint of weed. Shilpa shook her head. "It will relax you I can see you are tense and worried. Don't worry my dear I will not harm your lovely self. You are a desirable woman I have to say. Please try some with me," he held out the lit joint and she took a light puff and then another. He in turn took deep puffs and really let the smoke sink into the body.

Khan moved from his armchair to Shilpa on the sofa. She realized here comes the move. He ran his hand through her hair and then moved nearer to kiss her but she pulled her head back and made him rest against the back of the sofa. He had closed his eyes and was now snoring. Shilpa took the opportunity to walk out, signaled to the driver for the car and was in the hotel in thirty minutes.

The following evening she sat at the Embassy bar with Julian.

"This isn't going to be easy Julian. These guys are like dogs on heat and I know them if I give in now there will be nothing coming out of them. They would have got what they want and I will be discarded. Trust me I know," said Shilpa to the major as they had a soft drink in the bar. She explained to him this was a long-term assignment and she wasn't sure she wanted it after Khalid had spotted her.

After a hot chocolate drink she decided to have an early night even though the two generals had called her she didn't return their calls. As she entered the room she noticed a slip of paper on the floor. It said: *"Tomorrow morning you will take your breakfast in the coffee shop at 9 am and you will see me there. Sit on the table next to me with your back to my back."* No name. She knew who it was.

5
RETURN TO THE PAST

At 8.45 am Shilpa slipped into her caftan and went to the coffee shop where there was an African UN couple, a bald white man and two young women either NGO types or UN. There was no one else so she walked to an empty part of the café and sat down ordering a coffee and toast. At exactly 9 am Khalid entered the room in his traditional costume and flat hat and sat at the table next to Shilpa with his back to her.

"So I think you knew it was going to be me?" he whispered.

She didn't say a word. "I like the Americans and the Brits but we have to do business, you and I or else let me assure you will not leave this country alive or dead as they will never find you like the last six years. Are you ready to talk if so do not get up. I will leave and meet you in the garden near the dry fountain. If you do not agree walk away now."

Shilpa sat there for the next five minutes as Khalid left and walked to the area that must have been a breathtaking garden years ago. The old Mogul fountain was dry and crumbling. He sat on the edge and waited for Shilpa.

Ten minutes later she came and sat by his side. She remembered how he was one of the first men to rape her as Amjal offered her to him after a feast day. He had been so rough that she had a torn vagina, which took days to heal, and even during that period Amjal forced her into sex.

Shilpa's heart was beating like a motorbike engine. "What do you want?"

"Just to talk. We make small talk first then business OK? How you are and why you come back. You very stupid, like all woman, stupid," mumbled Khalid.

Long silence. "I have my life back Khalid so please don't do anything to me I beg you. I am not here to harm anyone just to do my project," said Shilpa.

"You think we are stupid Shilpa? You think the generals are all stupid? We all know you are not an expert on gardens- what you couldn't think of something better. Gardens in war torn Afghanistan! You people have good arms, soldiers, plenty money but politicians fucking stupid. No country has conquered us since Genghis Khan so what makes your people think they will own us? I hate Al Qaeda but they pay us good so we take them in. You see what will happen to you all soon. Now why you really here?"

"I just told you."

Wham! His hand flew through the air and slapped Shilpa on the cheek. Those green eyes of his seemed to tear through Shilpa like laser beams. "Don't forget who you talk to or I finish you here and no one touch me," he then smiled and used his hands in a beckoning way to say speak up.

Now there was another long silence.

"OK, but you promise not to touch me again, promise." He nodded. "Say it 'I promise on the grave of my mother.'"

"I promise on the grave of my mother I will not hurt you," mumbled Khalid.

"When the British caught us that day they interrogated both Abdul and myself and in the process they learnt from both of us about the drug trade and that is where the tribes of the Taliban made money and with whom. So when I got to London they helped me get better and in return asked me to come to Afghanistan again to help find the Americans and British who are involved in the drug trade. They know all of you are not involved but want to know who is within their own people."

"So why you go with Generals like whore?"

"Let's be clear about one thing Khalid I am not a whore and never was even when you people treated me like one. Stop using that word I really hate it."

Khalid was silent for a while then said, "What I get if I give you names? I know plenty. You think I know fuck nothing but I know fuck all."

Shilpa burst out laughing, "You probably do know fuck all of what I really need to know." The remark went right over Khalid's head.

"Right so we do business OK?"

"Yes Khalid we do business and you tell me all I need to know; you become rich man."

She stood up and gently waved Bye and walked away.

Back at the hotel she called Julian.

"Julian you are never going to believe what just happened" said Shilpa on the cell phone she had been given.

"What that you met with Khalid in the garden?"

"Oh Christ do you have eyes everywhere?"

"We are at war madam not a bloody cocktail circuit in Cannes. OK tell him you have secured a deal with him for 200 US dollars for every time he bring some really useful news to us."

"Jesus, you saw and heard the whole thing? Then why the hell didn't you come to my rescue when he slapped me?'

"Risks of the trade luv. Risks of the trade."

"So now what?"

"We follow a plan I have set up with London but we never thought this was going to happen and you do as you are told and in a few weeks you will be walking happily in Hyde Park you lucky thing you."

He is flirting she thought, cheeky monkey.

"So what's on tonight? More generals?"

"No the same one from two nights ago, A212. We call Aziz A212 for obvious reasons, good code too. You will meet him at a party and this time he says he wants 'quality time' with you. Actually used that phrase if you can believe it."

"Oh I can believe it. This isn't right I have to be a whore like Mata-Hari. One day they will make a film about me after I have been shot. I would rather make it with you Jules than with that pompous ape."

'Jules' is it now thought Julian. Well you never know life works in mysterious ways but I don't like the thought of that ape getting there first.

"Well 'Anita' why don't we give you some pills and you can do a Jerry Patel on him.

"My god how much do you know about me?"

"All there is to know." Julian smiled and clicked off the phone.

6
'ANITA' TAKES OVER

For the next ten days Shilpa as 'Anita' went out with Generals and Aziz Khan. In the course of meeting him she also saw a colonel and three brigadiers who all exchanged stories about the wild time they had with her but the truth was none of them did as 'Anita' wasn't putting it out which made the men even more lusty and hungry for her.

She noticed the weakest of all these was Brig. Walli Khan who was originally from Pakistan and now fighting against the Taliban but not thrilled with the Americans being there and had voiced his concerns so Shilpa decided to zero in on him, besides he was the best looking of all these guys.

The Brig's bungalow was smaller than the other ones she had been in but he was a bachelor, rare for a man in his forties and also had clearly had his share of ladies in his time in Pakistan if not here. 'Anita' asked to be shown around so when they finally reached the bedroom she held his hand and squeezed it. "Walli I know you know I see other officers but I just want to say I have never given in to any of them but you are someone special."

She pouted her lips at him and gently kissed him on the cheek then bit his bottom lip then opened his mouth with her tongue and mingled with his tongue for a full ten seconds before pulling away.

Walli just kept staring at her and slowly moved her over to the bed and gently laid her down and continued to kiss. It was a full hour before a knock on the door woke them up. They looked at each other and Walli covered 'Anita' with a sheet and got up to put his dressing gown on.

"Who is it?" he called out.

"Captain Haq sir I have a message for you it's urgent," came the reply.

Walli Khan carefully opened the door and stepped out so the officer couldn't see into the bedroom.

"I was taking a nap. What is it?"

"Sir we have spotted a band of Taliban's forces coming to the north fort of the city. The Americans have already moved but we couldn't find you so I have asked the men to fall in and I was wondering should I take them in sir?" asked the nervous Captain.

"Haq that is good. Yes we need to show the Americans we can also fight. Yes go and report to me afterwards. Yes go," said a confused Walli Khan. He was so engrossed with his newfound love that the battle twenty miles away was of no interest.

He walked back into the room and was so aroused to see 'Anita' with just a sheet between her naked legs that he pulled the sheet away and licked her all the way from her feet to her breasts and then bit her breast that made her genuinely scream with delight and she pulled his head and kissed him as he entered her again.

When it was over he lit a pipe and sat up in bed. What a foul smell it killed the real sexual thrill she had experienced a while back.

"What was all that about with that man at the door?" she asked

"Nothing to bother your pretty little head. Stroke me a bit with your mouth while I smoke I have always dreamt of this, please," he said puffing away.

She stroked his penis and took it deep in her mouth, which made him breath very heavily on the pipe, and soon he yelled out as he came in her mouth. She rushed to the bathroom to gargle and put some toothpaste on her finger and rub her teeth. He on the other hand had dropped his pipe on the floor and had gone to sleep.

'Anita' watched him for a while then decided she wouldn't leave the bed till she got what she had come for so after fifteen minutes she kissed his chest and woke him up. "Well tiger did I fulfill your fantasy?" she asked.

"Fulfill it? You past all expectations, amazing! You really haven't done this with any of the others?"

"No honestly. You really turn me on."

They opened a tin of sardines and the cook made some toast for them along with mutton sandwiches with mayo and mustard just like the clubs serve in Bombay and Karachi she thought.

"Walli why did you leave Lahore and come here?"

"I was stuck as a major for four years in the Pakistan army and the bastards were promoting juniors over me so I thought I would come here and they could use my expertise. Well they were bloody good to me and offered me a field rank at once and all that goes with it and so here I am but I will move up further in time. We are waiting to make our move," he said sipping his scotch.

"You are an exciting man Walli, one could fall for you easily. So do you get on with the likes of Hamid Khan and Aziz?"

"Oh yes we are just waiting out time as I said. It will come but the damn Americans are backing Karzai and it's not easy to fight them."

She poured more whisky into his glass as he was loosening up now.

"The Americans interfere everywhere and make a mess of it. Look at Iraq why on earth did they have to go there when Saddam was contained. Wait and see this will be Bush's biggest fiasco," said 'Anita.'

"You are quite political aren't you? Not something we see in women here."

Dinner was served at 10 pm and the two discussed politics, marriage, and the war stories of Brig: Walli Khan. Once it was over 'Anita' asked, "Would you like me to stay over tonight. I don't mind if it doesn't get you into trouble."

"Better not but I wouldn't mind another round in bed."

The round went on for just fifteen minutes as they were both full of food and drink and the energy had dissipated.

"Walli do you think you all can really oust Karzai. He comes across as a puppet of the Yanks never has anything to say that's worth a dime."

"Glad you noticed that. Most of us think the same but the army isn't ready to take on the foreign forces yet. We are waiting our time. Almost the entire army and what little we have in the air force want a strong man in charge who will tell you lot to get out and stay out for good."

Next morning Julian and two other officers from the embassy came to record every word that Shilpa had to report. This was dynamite! It was sent to London on a coded line within an hour of the meeting being over.

"Our girl has turned up trumps. By George she is something else," said the Director to Jill who just smiled and thought she is just doing what she always did before the Taliban got her. This was payback for her.

"Jill send her a message to say we are very pleased and to be careful. I want her to know we care about her," said the Director "I think we deserve a little tipple here. Sherry OK with you?"

Five thousand miles away 'Anita' was sitting with General Aziz in his gazebo lounging on the rich carpet, which felt like a thick mattress, with a cushion under her head and Aziz kissing her feet which he loved to do.

"I have to tell you in my whole life I have never met someone like you. I am so in love I can't even explain. I am a soldier, a fighting man not a poet but for you I do almost anything." He had moved to up to her hips and had pulled her long skirt over her waist and could now see her panties.

"I want to be someone important in life too Aziz. If I was to stay here with you would you marry me?"

Aziz stopped in his tracks. Marry? Is she mad?

"I, I don't know you really care for me? Then why we only make this sort of love and not full love? Let me be the reason you are up all night my love."

"You will be I always wake up when I have nightmares!"

"Oh, Oh you are too funny," laughed the general.

She just looked at him in the eyes and pulled her skirt over her head, then the white blouse that exposed her large round breasts. Slowly she undid the bra from the back and slipped it off. "Now take my panties off and kiss me there," she whispered in a husky voice.

Aziz just gulped and gulped he couldn't believe the sight in front of him. Never in his life had he seen anything so exquisite. He tried to take the panties down but fumbled and she pushed them over her ankles.

The general had gone limp through anxiety. He couldn't get it up. She played with him to no success. Shilpa actually felt sorry for him, as he had not forced himself on her since that first meeting. He got up from the carpet and went to cover himself with a bathrobe.

"This is the most shameful moment of my life. Please you cannot tell anyone."

The roar of laughter in Summers' office brought in others from the other rooms in the embassy. "What's so funny? Asked a young secretary.

"Believe it or not it's classified," said Julian.

"Invite him over to the hotel tonight and say you want to see if you can make things better. He will go for it," suggested one of the officers who had been seen but never introduced by name.

"Khalid left one of his notes he needs to see me. He suggest the gardens of Babur," said Shilpa.

The most famous place in Kabul was laid out by the Mughal ruler Babur in the early 16th century, and the site of his tomb; these gardens are the loveliest spot in the city. At 11 hectares, they are also the largest public green space but left to ruins during the war. Seeing the mess this masterpiece of landscaping brought genuine tears to Shilpa's eyes.

"So you are moved by gardens after all," said a voice she recognized from behind her. "I have been watching you for the last five minutes. You know I would like to be a tear on your face right now. You are and always were beautiful. I was wrong to treat you the way I did," said Khalid who was covered in a blanket from his head to his knees.

She told him about the deal that if he brought them good useful information he would get 200 Pounds each time and after that there might be a bonus if all went well for six months but it had to be useful and not something any Tom, Dick or Harry could find out. If any harm came to Shilpa the deal was off and the army would hunt him and the family down.

The man sat on the bench and thought for a while.

"500 Pound and not less," he blurted out.

"I am not in a position to make these deals I can only say what has been told to me," said Shilpa.

"500," he repeated and walked away.

As he was leaving the garden a Land Rover drove up to the gate and 2 soldiers jumped out and pushed Khalid into the back and drove off in a hurry, they didn't even look at Shilpa.

A light went on in the dark room where Khalid was sitting and a man walked in and slapped him on the face. "That was for Shilpa, what you did to her the other day. Now you greedy pig we offered you a very generous deal. More money than you have ever seen for you and your family and you make demands on us?"

The light was so strong in Khalid's face he couldn't see the face of the man talking to him. Two soldiers then came in and untied his hands from behind the chair and the lights came on in the room. Standing in front of Khalid was Major Julian Summers, that nice looking boy with impeccable manners and grace.

Behind the chair stood a corporal and a sergeant both built like brick houses and over six feet tall. There was no way Khalid, no slouch himself, would take on these two.

"Right, here is the deal. You don't perform we will hunt you down and kill you and your family and if you think I am joking just try me Khalid. Now because you were a greedy pig we will give you 100 pounds for each piece of information you bring us but if you do really well in 6 months I will promise you a house outside Kabul with four acres of land and a water well. This Her Majesty's government will promise you and you will not be asked to do any more work unless you want to earn money with us. Am I crystal bloody clear?" said Julian three inches away from his face.

Khalid spat in his face and then quick as lighting the sergeant knocked him on the floor and the corporal kicked him in the guts. Julian wiped the spit off his face, walked over to Khalid on the floor and lifted him by his shirt collar and punched him in the mouth, then on the nose and again on the mouth. Blood flowed all over Khalid's shirt and on the floor.

"Listen you swine you try that again you will never see your family or tribe again," said the sergeant. "We are here to help your country and you don't see that do you Mustafa or whatever your fucking name is? You think we want to be here you arsehole?" said the sergeant and hit him across the cheek and then let him slump to the floor. The three soldiers walked out of the room switching off the lights.

Julian didn't inform Shilpa as to what had happened. He just said they took him in for questioning. The army has very high quality, reconnaissance equipment and from 400 yards they could pick up every word that was being said by Khalid and Shilpa. Don't worry about him was all Julian said to her but she was worried. Julian didn't really know Khalid like she did.

The music was a Whitney Houston album on the hotel's audio system. On the double bed were General Aziz and his newfound love with whom he could consummate the relationship. "I tried to get that blue pill today but our doctors do not have it and I didn't want to ask the Americans. I am only 55 years old and have two children so it's not right this. What can you do 'Anita'?

She suggested they don't push it and just talk and then in time something will happen.

"Tell me general, I like that word –general- so powerful and sexy. Power is sexy right?"

"Oh yes no doubt about it '" replied the general.

In no time the conversation went to the politics of the country and as he drank more and more whisky he began to ramble but in the rambling was a lot of truth. How he was going to take over from the present President and rule with the army, a non-corrupt state and the first in Asia. Then rid the country of the Taliban and other Jihadist and make the country prosperous from its land wealth and build the big cites using the wealth for the people.

"I want to rule like your Lincoln said "A government of the people, by the people, and for the people." Not this rubbish puppet of the USA. They would never accept the corruption this place has in the USA or in UK. You people all think we are useless for allowing the Taliban to take over. Well some truth in that but let me tell you this is not a lot better. Everyday bombs go off killing hundreds of innocent people. You say we have free speech, where? Karzai has the police put anyone who speaks against him in prison."

The scotch bottle was over and he started on the gin. After more spouting about the corrupt regime he got out of bed and went to the bathroom and threw up. So disgusting thought Shilpa and I am expected to sleep with him. A shiver went up her spine. By this time she had names and places of the entire top rebel officers but Khan was not mentioned.

"I don't want to leave now people will think nothing happened between us so please let me sleep I will not hurt you my dear," his last words as the head hit the pillow he was out for the count. Shilpa dragged the duvet on to the floor with a couple of pillows and went to sleep. A hard bed was no stranger to her any more.

The detail messages were fired off to London and from there to the CIA in Langley outside Washington DC. Diane Kruger was now a senior Director of the middle and near east sections. When the classified memo came to her desk she almost screamed, "Shilpa More of India and beyond, my God!"

"What's happening boss?" said a junior of two-year service.

"You weren't here but. Oh my God this is too much…I can't believe this. Get me London and I want the Director in person," she said her head in a daze.

The Director filled her in but he too in turn was to learn a lot about Ms. Moray as the new spelling went. She was a viper in her days Kruger told the Director. She slept with everyone and did what it took to get this money laundering, arms dealing TV station from her own father and was there when the owner Jerry Patel was killed and covered up for it. She is no saint said Kruger; she is a piece of work!

"Well you have used her well Mr Director I must congratulate you. There are a few people in the USA who would love to hear this news am I free to talk?"

"Absolutely not. She is in great danger and this is very classified and now one of my most special agents." Kruger was dying to call the NJPD and tell them but she had to forget about it for the moment at least. The last they heard of Shilpa was when she went undercover as 'Shalini' with Salim to trade with the Taliban in Afghanistan and they lost the tracker there. No word from her for years so they presumed she had been killed.

The sun was hot this April morning when Julian came to see Shilpa at the hotel requesting her to come with him for a meeting with someone important. He drove her to the prison section of the base and then walked over to the high security cells. The three bolts on the door were opened and the light went on to see a sad specimen of man lying on the floor. He looked up at Shilpa with his tongue hanging out and he was breathing heavily.

"Khalid, Oh my God what's happen to him?" She turned to Julian who didn't say a word. She then noticed Khalid had chains on his ankles and they in turn were bolted to the wall.

"We need you to talk to him and tell him the deal we have given him is real and that he should take it," said Julian and walked out of the door leaving it ajar so he could enter in case of an emergency.

"Khalid, I don't know what deal they are talking about but these people are very serious and if they say what they have told you then they mean it," said Shilpa very worried at seeing him like this. "Listen to me I don't like any of you because of what you did to me and if that means they will kill or imprison you for life I don't give a damn but I will say I liked your wives and four children and I don't want to see them harmed and they will harm them make no mistake."

"You really believe that?" there was a long silence after Shilpa nodded her head.

"Alright I will do their dirty work and if they don't pay me I will come after you and if I don't someone else will and make no mistake of that miss fancy woman."

Shilpa walked out of the room and told Julian he was ready to do the bidding whatever it was, "and by the way if you cross him he and his tribesmen are coming after me. Thanks a lot, you are all bastards from the same whore mother," saying it she almost spat in his face, turned around and walked away.

When she got back to her room she wrote a letter to the Ambassador asking him to personally inform the chief of MI6 that she was off the assignment and she had more than paid for her rescue by the British army. She paid the hotel boy handsomely to deliver the message to the UK embassy.

The next day a call from the lobby asked her to come down urgently. An English woman in her twenties simply asked Shilpa to follow her into a car, which drove at speed to the UK embassy where Shilpa was walked, without a word, to the Ambassador's office.

"I am pleased to meet you. I have heard nothing but praise about your very sensitive work. I apologise for not having met you before but security forced me not to so now we meet," said a rather short man with heavy glasses who she knew was the ambassador. "Roland Howard at your service mam."

"Thank you sir for your kind words but I don't think any man can imagine what it's like to do what I have done and then to be made a bait for the bloody Taliban as I have now been made and that from a man who fucked me raw. Do you sir have any fucking idea what that is like to be torn in every single orifice of your body, do you sir?" Shilpa shouted and broke into tears. She collapsed on the leather Chippendale sofa. Howard didn't know what to do so he hesitated and then sat next to her and gently touch her arm.

"You are right I have absolutely no idea. I also have no idea how to make this up to you except to say you are a remarkable lady and the nation thanks you and I shall do my best to send you home soon," said a soothing Howard.

"Thank you sir, I have had enough now after six years with those people and then to be tricked into coming to Afghanistan by saying I was going to Iraq it's all too much."

"I am sorry I knew nothing of the Iraq situation I was told you had agreed to come here that's all."

"See you people lie just like them. You are no different because you wear fancy suits and ties and they wear flat hats and rough clothes you really are all the same. You know sir you will never get them to be you. One day you will leave because they will never let you dominate them, couldn't do it a hundred years ago and you won't do it now; more than that you are in bed with them for drugs and that is the most shocking thing of all. You lot kill your own people back home!"

"I think this calls for a nice cup of tea for us to simmer down and talk sense. What say you?"

Bloody tea that's the Brit answer to the world's problems isn't it. Tea!

Shilpa shook her head in disbelief and started to admire the ceiling, which had a fresco on it.

A knock on the door brought in some Earl Grey tea, chocolate cover bath Oliver biscuits from Fortnum and Masons still in the round tin and a delicious fruit cake possibly from the same royal grocer. Howard was a cleaver man and he tried to divert the subject to talk about his family still in the UK and the problems he was having with his nineteen year old rebel daughter.

"What advice would you have for my wife and I? I really mean it we are at our wits end with her drugs, dozen boys a month and I'm sure she sleeps with all of them, I mean I am not narrow-minded. I am a child of the 60s and good lord we got up to some high jinks. You'd be shocked Shilpa but this rampant use of drugs and bonking, pardon my French, spending money like there is no tomorrow. I am not a lord with an inheritance I have worked my way up the ladder on a civil servants pay," said Howard now trying to divert Shilpa from her worries.

"How much time do you spend with her?" asked Shilpa

From there they went into his life and how he came up the ladder and married for position and not love but then he assumed Shilpa coming from India knew all about that stuff and how do they deal with it in India and so on. The time over two hours had passed and the staff was left wondering if something more than talk was going on in there.

A knock on the door brought all that to a halt and Julian entered. "'Morning Shilpa, Good morning sir. Have you told her about …"?

"No, No I haven't had a chance…"

"Well you have been in here for almost two hours sir.."

"Bloody cheek, who the hell do you think you are talking to Major? How dare you sir talk to me like that? Get out!" No one had ever heard Roland Howard lose his temper like that. His secretary, the girl who accompanied Shilpa, ran into the room as Julian was leaving. "What's happened sir?"

"Miss Shilpa and I will have lunch in the quarters today and get the chef to come up with some smoked salmon, cream cheese and bagels. I want my traditional Jewish breakfast. Oh and some of that fine Turkish coffee, you know the one I like?"

She simply nodded and walked out quick time.

"I have some work in other departments and you look like you could do with a nap. So make yourself at home and I will see you in a couple of hours."

Shilpa was sleepy and very emotional so she lay down on the Chippendale and tried to read an old Daily Express but it sank to her chest and she was fast asleep.

7
TITO

"Jill have you seen the fax from Kabul our lady is breaking down. Not good, not good at all we have to have her there for the big one. Shall we give her an R & R in the south of France and meet her father?"

"No sir we will never see her again. She likes sex sir, I know who doesn't… but she needs it and not from these bores she has been with. Let's give her some real romance for a week and then spring it on her. I have an idea sir," said Jill.

The Hilton bar in London is a great pick up joint for the rich and the elderly. Yes the elderly as gigolos frequent it and so do mature call girls. Jill, in her forties, made herself look available. It wasn't long before a skinny youth approached her and offered her a drink. "Thanks but no thanks" said Jill and toyed with her gin and tonic.

After an hour she began to wonder if the stories of this bar were true when in came Romano, well he would be called Romano wouldn't he? 5'-10," Latin looking with dark hair and a thin top lip but a full bottom one. Umm, could be George Clooney in a darker skin thought Jill. Wonder if he can talk.

He sat near her but didn't say a word. Jill knocked her glass over and the gin touched his blazer. "Oh I am so sorry. Let me pay for the cleaning," she gushed.

"It's Ok I am used to it that's why I wear this old blazer it's had gin. Scotch, vodka, juices and you name it spilt on it over the years and I am still wearing it; my good luck charm. Romano is my name and you lovely lady?" he oozed greasy charm from every pore. Don't know thought Jill but may be good in bed who knows. Let's see.

After a few drinks and life in Tuscany, small town call Cortona, where he was born and lived running a café in the main street. "One day I would like to take you there. So beautiful but not much work. Its thousands of years old you know, the Etruscans first came there and the walls are 3000 years old and the views from my house is to die for, like a renaissance painting by Da Vinci," gushed the Italian.

"Would you like to see the view from my room it looks over the Kings road and lovely sites of red buses passing by and people pouring out of pubs at this time of night. It's really lovely," she said smiling.

"I love red buses but let's go faster than any bus, by cab," he said and winked at her.

Needless to say she paid for the cab knowing MI6 will pick up the tab.

When they reached the bedroom he made her turn her back to him and slowly knelt at her feet and lifted her dress running his hands up to her bottom and then feeling her in front, moving his fingers into her panties and stroking her very gently and then slowly inserting his fingers into her and tickling the clit. Jill just stood very still and kept taking deep breaths and hoping this would never end. It had been ages since she had been with a man, perils of the job.

It was hot that Friday morning as Jill got to work. She was hot all right. Mind blowing night and one she had not experienced since she was in college when she was seduced by the Psych professor. She walked into the boss' office and announced she had her man for Shilpa and he was so broke that he would do anything for Queen and country even if they weren't his own.

Over the next four weeks Romano del Filimo was trained to be a spook by one of the most famous spy agency in the world, the MI6. He loved it as he really was going to play a James Bond type of part and that in a country unknown to him as yet. First he was to get in shape, really fit not just look sexy in his clothes, then a course in firearms and some Karate. Ten hours a day was his schedule just for the physical and then four hours studies the Middle East and Afghanistan. That was when he began to guess his destination. Crash course in Arab and Afghan etiquette and some local knowledge. No messing around with local women was his strict brief.

"Romano we know a lot about you so don't fool around. You have had a useless life so far besides screwing around with "mature women" and a few younger ones but what your shrink test did reveal is you are very resourceful, your reactions are excellent and your street sense is above normal, you are extremely street wise. We also know you came to the UK when you were twenty-two from Sicily and not Tuscany. You worked as a sort of hit man cum goffer for a local Don. The Italian police say you have at least two murders on your hands. We don't give a damn but you cross us and we will hand you over before you can say "Mama Mia," said Jill.

"So you are now in the SIS or MI6 working for Britain your adopted country and you will be paid government salary of 120 Pounds a week and some expenses, which you have to account for. A weapon will be issued and you can use it in extreme life and death situation it's not a "License to kill" anyone. You will now be known are Tito Lanza and will answer to that name. Why that name you may well ask, well I am an opera fan and I loved Tito Gobi the greatest baritone of all time and I was drawn to opera by Mario Lanza's films hence you are now Tito Lanza. In two days' time you will go to an airport somewhere in England where you will be given your destination and all the details you need to know. You will spend one day studying them in the local hotel and then fly out the next night. Any questions?

"Yes where is my money to be paid to me if I am not here. I need to know if it's safe."

"Your money will be in an off shore bank in the Channel Island so you won't pay taxes and as far as the IRS is concerned you do not exist. Now good luck and seriously take care of yourself Tito," said Jill giving him a hug and a light kiss on the cheek.

72 hours after that conversation Tito was on a vintage VC10 bound for Kabul. These aircrafts from the 1960s were brought back into service as the RAF had to fly over 200,000 men to Afghanistan a year from Brize Norton. In his notes he was told he had to meet up with a fellow agent and *"make sure you do everything to make her happy and satisfied. Do whatever it takes and safe-guard her at the same time she is a VIA–very important agent."* He was to meet her accidently and make it clear he was not SIS or for that matter there to meet her.

His other job was to mingle with the brass as a playboy type working for a British firm looking for mining opportunities in the country. The sort of chap who would promise the top brass a good time when they came to London and did he know some great places!

For the first two days in Kabul he only met Major Julian Summers and a few people at the embassy including the SIS head who was a quiet middle-aged man but had been in the service for over 30 years. Most people called him Sam but few knew that was not his real name. He briefed Tito on Shilpa and told him about her movements so he could accidently bump into her in a day or so.

In the meantime Shilpa was still working her way through the rest of the Afghan army as one sport put it but she was amazing at getting the information as no one else had done. Two days after Tito had arrived in Kabul she noticed the handsome Italian in the coffee shop reading a paper.

"Hi anyone sitting with you?" she asked

"No, please take a seat I don't know any one so have to sit alone. I am Tito Lanza here to look into some mining opportunities and you?" he said very casually.

"Oh I am Anita here to do a long series on TV and a book on gardens."

"Really how interesting. All I know is roses and lilies," smiled Tito.

They drank their coffee and ate the rather coarse bread that was served that day. It varied from day to day and today there were no eggs or even cornflakes. He said he was here for a few weeks and they should meet up and she could show him Kabul. Quite a hunk she thought to herself. Yes sir you're my baby, very soon.

Shilpa played 'hard to get' for a couple of days didn't want to show how desperate she was for a really good handsome lover then one day she saw him in the book stall and went up and asked how he was etc. "Doing anything tonight? She asked.

"I may have plans but not sure. Why you free for dinner?" he asked

BOOM-Bang a massive explosion went off in the garden. Smoke and fires were burning and people screaming and shouting. Tito immediately put his arm around Anita and tried to get to the stairs but another bomb went off in the lobby and an arm came flying through the air and hit Anita in the face that made her scream. The lobby was full of smoke and some fire by the main reception desk.

Siren sounded and a group of soldiers from the ISAF forces came in and told people not to panic. Tito and Anita now couldn't even see the steps as the black smoke took over the lobby. He held on to Anita's arm and tried to guide her to where he thought the stairs were. The smoke was now choking people and the place was full of men and women coughing and spluttering, fortunately there were no kids in the place.

In a small clearing Tito spotted the staircase and made a move towards it. They ran up to the third floor where the smoke was less dense and looked down to see if they could help anyone. They saw the legionnaires from France lifting bodies and some people screaming as they came across body parts.

He then moved to the fourth floor as they went up one more flight he rushed into his room. It was smokeless but warm, as the AC had been knocked out. The morning sun was streaming through the window when they spotted each other in the mirror they started to smile. Both their faces were black and their clothes would have to be thrown away. Tito went to the window to look out and saw people dead on the driveway, cars mangled, and the dry fountain completely destroyed, just a few sections of concrete remaining. Anita tried the phone but it was dead.

Suddenly there was gunfire and then more and more, looking out of the window they saw the Taliban fighters ripping up the walls of the hotel with their AK 47s and throwing grenades from the far side of the garden.

The French forces were very quick to reply and within five minutes the Americans and British troops arrived which made the Taliban retreat and run but in the process losing several of their men who were shot in the back while running away.

This was not in Tito's plan to seduce Anita who he knew was really Shilpa.

8
THE ATTACK

It took the authorities most of the day to just clear the smoke and the damaged areas so people could move around slowly and not trip over the debris. The Afghan politicians came to see the damage led by the president who was stunned that an international hotel would be attacked in broad daylight, a complete failure of security forces from all sides. Media coverage was limited as most of them were in the hotel and had trouble getting to their equipment and even if they did the atmosphere was so dense with smoke nothing much could be filmed.

Tito sat on the sofa in his room while Anita went to the bathroom to clean herself with the trickle of water that was coming out of the taps. She washed her face and then realized that her body was a mess to say nothing of her clothes. Tito in turn had never experienced anything like this and was in a mild shock whereas Anita had been a target of many American and ISAF bomb attacks from the air.

She looked out of the window and saw the hotel staff and some soldiers cleaning up the mess below and so decided to go to her room. Tito refused to let her go alone so he followed her up another set of stairs to the fifth floor where the damage was minimum. In her room she notice the water flowed better so she told Tito to wash up and put on a bath robe which he promptly did and then came out and lay on the bed while Anita cleaned herself and changed into a pair of jeans and a T-shirt.

"Now what do we do?" she asked.

Tito walked around the room and looked out of the window a couple of times thinking they didn't train me for this in London last month. He opened the mini bar and took out two small bottles of brandy, which were only served to foreigners, he didn't bother about a glass and handed one to Anita and took a long swig from his bottle, then just sat there thinking.

"Let's go downstairs now the smoke is lifting," he said quite clueless as to what should be done.

Downstairs they worked their way through the rubble and the soldiers clearing up the bodies scattered amongst the furniture and concrete when they came across the top half of the body of the young receptionist they dealt with every day. Anita threw up on the spot and Tito had to rush her outside for so called fresh air. A Range Rover drove up and out jumped Julian Summers who saw the couple, "Are you two alright? Sorry I couldn't get away trying to arrange for the injured and dead we wondered if you would be among them. Thank God you are OK," he said breathing heavily and looking ten years older.

Julian packed them into the RR and off they went to the embassy where two small rooms had been arranged for them. After a shower and some fresh clothes for Tito they were given a debriefing by the staff as to what happened at the hotel. At the end of which a large card was brought in to show Tito and Anita, written in someone's blood it said: *FREE KHALID NOW OR YOU WILL ALL DIE NEXT TIME."*

"I also think it's time we told you two who you really are. Tito this is Shilpa but outside these walls she is still Anita to you. Shilpa this is Tito and he is with the firm not a commercial traveller. You need to watch each other's backs and Tito is trained in the use of arms and is going to be taking care of you in every way," said Julian with a smile. "We have a task for you now and then Shilpa you both return to London."

Over the next hour they sat with the team and heard what they had to do. Later they had a good night's rest.

This June morning as Shilpa got in the Range Rover (RR) she realized she had been in Afghanistan for 63 days and it seemed like 63 years to her. Tito got in beside her and said "Well let's get this over with ASAP and get back to the land of the living," he patted her leg and then squeezed her hand just to let her know he was there for her.

Twenty minutes later they stopped at the base prison where she saw Khalid being marched out in chains on his feet and arms then being made to sit in a Land Rover, which was going to accompany them with two armoured Warrior vehicles and eight men from the crack special force unit. Into Shilpa's Range Rover jumped Major Julian Summers in full battle uniform and told Shilpa to get ready to confront Khalid and tell him what was about to happen.

She walked over to Khalid's Land Rover and got in beside him. He didn't stir a muscle although he must have been surprised to see her. She didn't raise her voice but softly said:

"Listen Khalid I am going to make this short OK? As you must know we had a major bomb attack in your name but it seems it was a diversionary tactic to do what they really wanted to do which was to steal arms. An Afghan army Special Forces commander has defected to an insurgent group allied with the Taliban in a Humvee truck packed with his team's guns and high-tech equipment."

Khalid acted as if he had no interest in what was being told to him so Shilpa then said, "It was General Hamid Khan, who raided the supplies with his 20-man team in the capital that day of the bombing. He may be the first Special Forces commander to switch sides, joining the Hezb-e-Islami organization. All this supposedly in your name, now you are going to lead us to him and if you play games your wives and four kids, who are being watched by a group of soldiers, will be killed one by one for every mistake you make." Khalid spat in her face; Shilpa in turn slapped him across the mouth and spat in his face.

"Enough you two. Khalid you show disrespect to her again in any way and I will let two of my men loose on you and you have no idea how much they want to kick you to death," shouted Julian. "Now we will drive out of town and you lead us to the hiding place if not I will break your fingers one at a time," he took Khalid's thumb and bent it till he actually made a sound of pain.

The terrain is rocky, red-brown and rugged with nothing but boulders, sand and wind to keep you company. The platoon drove slowly as the place is littered with mines and in many places land mines from the time of the Russian occupation in the early 80s. Khalid knew this so his vehicle was the first in line as he was someone who cherished his life if not the others.

"You see that rock on the left, so when you get there stop because there are mines in that field. You need to get your sappers out to sweep the area," said Khalid.

Two hundred yards up they stopped and four sappers jumped out to sweep the place. This gave the people in the armoured vehicles a chance to discuss strategy and have a cup of tea, the English answer to everything.

The sappers started to set up the "Bangalore Torpedo" – which was first devised by Captain McClintock, of the British Indian Army unit of the Madras Sappers in Bangalore, India, in 1912. He invented it as a means of exploding booby traps and barricades left over from the Boer and Russo-Japanese Wars. The Bangalore torpedo would be exploded over a mine without the sapper having to approach closer than about 3 meters. The Bangalore Torpedoes are currently manufactured by Mondial Defense Systems of Poole, UK and for US armed forces as the M1A2 version.

Khalid was surprised to see this devise being used, he thought the men would go out on foot and use mine detectors, he spilled the mug of tea he had been given and the sergeant next to him noted he was nervous.

"What's the matter, you nervous? Don't worry our boys know what they are doing," said the sergeant.

"Don't they use mine sweepers? This not good they bring rocks down and block road," said Khalid.

"Sir," yelled out the sergeant. "Khalid here has a point sir, he feels the explosion from the Banger will bring the rocks down and block the road."

"Hey you sappers be bloody careful and don't bring the damn boulders down and block the road," yelled the lieutenant to the men on the ground.

It was too late the men fired the torpedo and it created a massive explosion with mines going off and rocks tumbling down on to the path and on to the vehicles.

There was dust and smoke everywhere and then a silence and as the smoke cleared then a barrage of gunfire came from the mountain, which caught the platoon by surprise. The sun was shining straight into the eyes of the soldiers and there was no way to tell where the rapid rifle fire was coming from.

Three of the sappers lay dead; the armoured cars were firing in all directions blinded by the sun. Shilpa crouched close to the captain, her throat like sandpaper and her heart beating like a marathon runner.

"What the hell is happening?" she called out.

"We have been led into an ambush by that bloody man. I am going over to break his fucking thumb!" said the captain. He opened the hatch of the LR and dodging bullets ran to the vehicles with Khalid in it and jumped in.

"You son of a bitch. The major bloody warned you didn't he about messing us up?" he shouted at Khalid and took his handcuffed left hand and pulled his left thumb back till he heard it snap and Khalid screamed over the gun fire. "Next time I am going to cut off your fucking cock!"

The sergeant, corporal and two privates were dumbstruck. "Sir you can't do this to him," said the corporal.

"Do what corporal? I didn't do anything he struck his hand when the vehicle jerked in the fighting. Now get the hell out of here by going back for eight hundred yards so we can regroup. Right sergeant?" said the captain.

"Whatever you say sir. Right, you heard the officer corporal get moving," shouted the sergeant.

The LR turned around and was followed by all the others for the next half-mile. The firing ceased and the officers jumped out to confer.

"Why did you leave your vehicle captain?" asked Julian who was the senior officer.

"To fulfill your wishes sir, but I noticed that Khalid had already broken a thumb when we came under fire. I think he is in some pain now sir,' said the captain.

"Right, so now what's the plan is he going to cooperate?" asked Julian.

"Well I told him next time we come under any fire he may lose his cock sir," smiled the captain.

"Right. Alright listen we are going back and going around the mountains they won't expect us to do that as it going to add a day to our little junket. OK so let's go," said Julian very much in command.

The convoy took the detour and drove for over thirty miles to get to the other side of the mountain. Finally at sunset they pitched tents and secured the camp to eat their rations and take a nap till sunrise. Four soldiers took it in turns to keep watch for two hours at a time. The medic put Khalid's hand in a splint and gave him a shot of morphine.

The sun rises on the Chinese boarder of Afghanistan and the clock jumps three and a half hours. It's the biggest time difference between neighbouring countries; as China in 1949 gave itself the same time zone for the entire country rather like the British did in India.

Within thirty minutes, of the sun hitting the tents, the platoon was on its way having had its "char" and biscuits. When Shilpa saw the splint on Khalid's left hand it brought a smile to her face and she was thinking I would like to do that to his cock, which had violated her many times.

Tito had been keeping a very low profile as he knew he was out of his depth and wasn't even sure why he was here, certainly not to seduce Shilpa under these circumstances.

For the next four hours the convoy seemed to be going in whatever direction Khalid told them to go to find the tribe. He had realized by now these English were not there to play a game of cricket.

They were in the central Highlands, which cover almost two thirds of the country; the main area being the "Hindu Kush" known as the *Valley of Death*, which has seen more blood than any other part of the nation. The highest point in the Hindu Kush is Tirich Mir at 25,289 ft. in Chitral District of Pakistan.

To the east the Hindu Kush buttresses the Pamir range near the point where the borders of China, Pakistan and Afghanistan meet, after which it runs southwest through Pakistan and into Afghanistan, finally merging into minor ranges in western Afghanistan.

As the convoy navigated itself through the narrow roads made by previous expeditions and old trade routes they came across river crossings and steep mountain terrains. The going was slow and tedious as the amoured cars get hot inside and the Land Rovers were not allowed to use the air conditioning to save fuel. As the sun was setting Shilpa grew restless and very uncomfortable.

"This is more than I signed up for you know. Julian this isn't fair," groaned Shilpa.

"Life isn't fair you surely have figured that out by now Shilpa," said Julian.

"You can say that again," said Tito who had been cramped next to the private in charge of the radio.

Boom! Machine gun fire! Boom another bomb. The ground shook and it made Shilpa grab Julian's arm. Tito put his arm around Shilpa and pulled her towards himself. The vehicle shook again as if in an earthquake.

Julian leaned out to see the mortars were hailing down on the platoon and the firepower from the rifles came from the semi-circle of peaks surrounding the British but the platoon was firing back and moving at a high rate of knots because the Warrior infantry-fighting vehicle has the speed and performance to keep up with Challenger 2 main battle tanks over the most difficult terrain, and the firepower and armour to support infantry in the assault.

Warrior infantry command and section vehicles are fitted with a turret mounted 30mm Rarden cannon that will defeat light armoured vehicles out to a range of 1500m, an 8x magnification image-intensifying night sight and eight 94mm light anti-armour weapon heat rockets. These were fired at will at the enemy targets as the platoon could see in the evening light thanks to the night vision capabilities of the Warrior.

"Khalid mate I think your cock is about to be broken now," said the sergeant.

"No. Please no I did not know about this I swear I did not know, please believe me," pleaded Khalid. "We are only about half an hour from the village now."

The sergeant got on to the radio with the firing still continuing and called out "Sir the man says we are only thirty minutes from the destination. I think he is being truthful as he is scared he will lose his cock," joked the sergeant under fire.

Julian and the captain looked out of the Warriors and saw the firing from the opposition was slowing down and they were barging through with the dust being kicked up and with the sun setting it was hard for the enemy to see where they were firing. Whereas the British had them in their sights surgically taking them out. In the distance about two miles away they could see the lights of a village. The people there must have heard the gun fire and the bombs so the platoon decided to camp behind some small peaks so as not to be spotted. The night was cold but they were ordered not to light any fires and they would go in just before dawn.

At 5.30 am the major gave the order for the convoy to move out and they knew the drill on arrival. Within twenty minutes the convoy arrived a hundred yards from the first house of the settlement allowing the soldiers to go into action.

In complete silence the entire village was surrounded in less than five minutes. The captain looked at Julian who nodded and he fired the flare gun in the air.

Twelve soldiers rushed into the designated houses, then without a shot being fired, within minutes had the members of the tribe walk out into the courtyard.

Shilpa was escorted out of the RR and brought to face them. Her stomach was churning and her blood pressure was at 140. She walked towards them slowly but then realised they didn't recognise her new image and in army uniform. The lieutenant and corporal from the second Warrior walked over with Khalid who had his face covered with a scarf.

"Now is this the lot of them?" asked Julian to the captain.

"Yes sir. Shilpa can you ID this lot as your gang?"

She walked up to them and saw in their eyes that some of them were suspicious of her. Didn't they know her from somewhere? Suddenly she stopped and her jaw dropped. She turned around and walked back in double time to Julian.

"My God he is here. Khalid lied; he was not hanged, the bastard lied again," whispered Shilpa.

"What are you talking about?" asked Julian.

"Amjal Khan he is here at the back with the shawl over his head trying to look like a woman. He is the bloody leader who kidnapped me and raped me for 6 years. You have to take him in now," said Shilpa.

Julian whispered to the captain who in turn quietly gave an order; within minutes women and children were moved to the left and the men on the right. Shilpa noticed Amjal had moved with the women so she whispered to Julian and he walked up to Amjal, drew his weapon and pointed it at his head then with the nod of his head said 'move it.' Amjal stood still and stared at Shilpa, she realised he had recognised her.

"What for you bring this bitch here? I save her life and made her my wife and now she betrays me and my people who loved her," said Amjal then spat on the ground towards Shilpa.

A hum in the sky distracted everyone; two giant Merlin helicopters were flying in at 160 knots towards the village. They landed and four Marines jumped out of each one and ran towards the group on the ground. Within ten minutes the men were moved into the choppers with their hands cuffed behind their backs and black hoods over their heads, except Amjal who was being held by Julian and three members of his platoon.

Seeing the choppers take off into the morning sun Julian and the captain turned their attention to Amjal and brought forth Khalid who still had a scarf over his head and had not witnessed any of the action that morning.

"Lieutenant bring our man here. Take off the cover and let him see his friend," said Julian.

Khalid and Amjal stared at each other unable to say a word. Amjal spat in Khalid's face and Khalid who was handcuffed tried to release himself but his arms were secured.

"Do you know this man Khalid?" asked the captain.

"Yes he is Amjal Khan, the leader of this tribe and is a Taliban chief."

"Shilpa do you know this man and is Khalid correct?"

"Yes he certainly is and he is the man who raped me for six mind-boggling years."

A squad was formed that marched Amjal to one of the huts. Julian, a sergeant and two burly privates walked in behind him. In about two minutes one could hear some groans and then some yells and within five minutes screaming pain.

Shilpa wanted to watch but the captain held her back.

The platoon settled down to some breakfast, again four men were on watch but the rest brewed tea and opened up their rations: The UK one consists of a cardboard square box with three "boil in a bag" meals, dessert, a snack, and a brew kit for coffee or tea. When you're on the ground and you're tucked up at night into some foreign Afghan compound, the one piece of morale and nourishment you have for the day is what comes in this silver bag. So what exactly you find when you open it up makes a huge difference in your state of mind.

Ninety minutes later the talking stopped as they saw a bloody body of Amjal being half dragged out of the hut. He couldn't stand up on his own, his face was covered in blood and his robes were open and one could see the bruising on his chest and stomach. They hadn't got much out of him about General Khan and his group. The only thing they got out of him was he had escaped from the jail in Kandahar.

"Christ almighty what have we become!" said a corporal.

"Shut up lad. I don't want to hear a sound from you again till we get back and perhaps not even then. Now belt up," said the sergeant in a firm and low voice.

Tito who had been cowering by the Land Rover the entire time came out to see what was going on. Even when the soldiers had their breakfast he ate his rations quietly on his own. He had vomited earlier and tried to sleep when all others were waiting to see what had happened to Amjal Khan.

"When are we going back? I am not well," said Tito.

"Now Tito, now. We are going home. Let's move it," ordered Julian.

9
THE NEW LIFE

When Shilpa and Tito saw the lobby of the hotel in Kabul they simply smiled at each other knowing they were back safely. Tito looked appealing to Shilpa in his sweatshirt, tight jeans and five-day stubble. It had taken them two days of moving very fast to get back to base from the village without seeing any opposition. The service at the reception was slow as there were ISAF officers and civilians ahead of them.

"What I would give for some good food and a fuck right now is anybody's guess," muttered Shilpa.

"Give me time to shower and shave and then maybe I will oblige you with one of your wishes madam," whispered Tito.

Shilpa stuck her tongue out at him and wiggled it to say OK.

Twenty minutes after they reached their respective rooms there was a knock on Shilpa's door. "It's open come in," she said.

In walked Tito; clean-shaven with a splash of Gucci cologne in a white shirt open to the navel and fresh pair of jeans that he wore without any underwear that made his intent very obvious.

Shilpa was sitting having a meal still in her grubby uniform and a bit smelly from the trip. "Wow you were in a hurry. Aren't you hungry?" she asked.

"Only for you darling," he said and licked his upper lip.

"Oh please not that corny line you'll spoil the effect. It may work on some silly women but not me. Let me have a shower and then you can do your best work."

She stepped in the shower and then sat down on the floor and let the hot water cascade over her. The force of the water massaged her enervated body and she found herself thinking of the days roaming with the Taliban. When she finally appeared in a bathrobe from the bathroom Tito was fast asleep on the bed, she hadn't realized she had been in there for over thirty minutes and he was dog-tired. She went to the other side of the bed put her head on the pillow and fell asleep in less than a minute.

The phone rang right next to Shilpa's ear, which made her wake up with a start.

"Hello. Who? What is it Julian?" she was really annoyed.

"Just checking if you are OK. I can't get hold of Tito any idea where he is?"

"No not a clue I need to get back to sleep. Good night," she said hanging up the phone only to see it was only 7 pm; she'd been asleep for three hours.

She turned to see Tito peacefully fast asleep with his back to her. His neck and shoulders were bare where the shirt had come off, she kissed his back and then his neck with her left hand she touched his crotch and there she felt him come alive but he just grunted and moved his legs to say 'leave me alone.'

"Tito I need you," she whispered in his ear and then ran her tongue inside his left ear, which made him wake up and turn over. She looked at his beautiful face and kissed him on the lips at the same time unzipped his jeans only to realize he had no underwear. She moved her head from his mouth to his groin and took him in deep. It had been years since she had taken a man in her mouth, as the Taliban didn't like the practice, thank God.

Tito took off her bathrobe and turned her on her back, gently licked her nipples and then bit them playfully. She frolicked with him and then he entered her, which made her gasp then she moved like she hadn't done in years. The sex was wild and wonderful for the next forty minutes. She called out "Come with me I am coming, come!"

His mouth wide open Tito exploded inside her and then collapsed on top of her wet body.

"Oh my God! Did I need that!" she said and repeated herself several times.

"You are really something else Shilpa; *cara mia. Tu sei molto speciale,*" he said with a very sincere look.

"Thank you Tito you are good I have to say and you made my day, no my year. Sleep well," she said panting heavily and turned over to dream the rest of the night away.

London was thrilled to hear from Tito that he had calmed Shilpa down so that she was willing to stay on for a few more weeks. Tito became her nightly companion and also her bodyguard. One evening as they were leaving the hotel lobby an Afghan came up to her and said, "You bitch you will get your just rewards on earth not in heaven for betraying your husband," then slapped her face.

Tito who was a few feet away talking to a US officer saw this and sprang to her defense. He got the man by the throat with his left hand and hit him with his right fist. He then forced the man to the floor and hammered his fist into him several times. The American officer had also seen the incident so didn't do anything noticing Tito had the upper hand then after the Afghan took a battering he pulled Tito off the man and beckoned two security men to come and arrest the Afghan. It turned out he was Amjal's cousin and had known Shilpa in her captive days.

"You are not safe here Shilpa. You have to go back now," said Tito. He called London and told Jill they were playing with her life and it was not fair as she had done her share of the bargain and it was time to let her off. Shilpa's libido had gone down and her interest in sex took a back seat. She even asked Tito to sleep in his own room now and all she wanted was to get back home to London.

Two days later she and Tito were on a USAF Boeing 707 out of Kabul to London.

Their arrival in London was in the fog and the plane was landed on autopilot. The weather was dreary and wet but she was "home" and that's all that mattered now. She looked at Tito in the hanger of the RAF station, no clue where she had landed to say is this it? He held her hand and kissed her gently on the lips.

"I will see you again soon. This is no longer just a job," he said kissing her ear lobe and smiling.

When the car reached St. Mary's Mansions in Maida Vale, by the canal, she rushed up the stairs instead of going by the lift and opened the door to find a sweet smell of lavender and the lights on. She stood in the hallway and took in her bags the driver that brought up and then collapsed on the carpet crying her eyes out and her whole body was shaking. As she pulled herself together she was reminded of the old Indian proverb; *"Before we can see properly we must first shed our tears to clear the way."*

Shilpa walked to the bedroom and her mind went back to India and her family. What was she going to do now?

The following morning she was woken up by the phone it was Jill telling her they were sending a car for her to come to the MI6 offices as the Director wanted to speak to her. Ninety minutes later Shilpa entered the Director's office to be told that her days with MI6 were over as she had helped capture Amjal and Khalid. The former was going to Guantanamo Prison in Cuba and Khalid was being held in an Afghan prison in Kabul. The irony was that Amjal was a lad carrying guns and taking messages for the CIA during the Russian occupation in Afghanistan when the Taliban was being encouraged by the USA. They created a monster, which they were now fighting.

He also told Shilpa that she would have to leave her flat in ninety days and would be compensated with fifty thousand pounds and a ticket to anywhere she wanted to go. "You should go to lunch with Jill who will fill you in with the details of your departure from us just a lot of boring paper work, sorry Shilpa but I want to thank you because even you don't know how much information we now have thanks to your efforts. Good bye," he said with genuine sadness in his voice.

Jill was eating her pate and toast whilst Shilpa had order smoked salmon and a cucumber salad. "So what are you going to do with your life now this part is all over?" asked Jill after she had filled Shilpa in with the boring formalities of leaving the service.

"I would love to know what happened to my family and the friends I knew years ago, in another life," she said.

"Well I have been asked to fill you in about your family for starters. Your father is in the south of France married to a younger woman who used to act in his TV serials. Your mother is in Mumbai, it's what they now call Bombay but the courts and the stock exchange are all still 'Bombay.' Sadly she had not been well. We had someone check on her while you were away and it seems she is living with her sister and family. You should go and see your father first. We checked him out and he is in Cannes where his boat is docked but they, I think the wife's name is Shalini, they are staying in a hotel at night and come on board in the day to entertain guests."

"You people are amazing! Did you do this for me or for yourselves?"

"Both I guess. We always need info and well as the Director said you have a ticket to anywhere you want to go. May I suggest you take a flight to Paris, Nice, Paris and then where ever the hell you want to go," said Jill with a warm smile and held Shilpa's hand for a few seconds.

"Tell me more please. What happened to Ashok Kapoor the film star and then there was Darius Cooper his friend where are they?"

"Well Kapoor killed himself after he was released from jail. There was a public outcry for his early release but he became a TV game host but his wife and family broke up with him so he took his life the day before 9/11. As for Darius Cooper he is a teacher, I believe, in San Diego."

"Oh my God! He killed himself, Wow! And Darius is he married?"

"I believe so to a teacher I think; Diane, or Dena something like that. Why you interested in him?'

"Its Dalia and well I was once interested in him. I don't suppose I am even a blip on his radar today."

"Shilpa please take my advice and go to Cannes make up with your father it will do you a lot of good and let us find out if it's safe for you to return to India. Then as I said you have a ticket to anywhere so then go to America if you so wish but see your dad first."

As Shilpa was on the payroll of the service for another ninety days she didn't rush off after all she had a beau in London now. Tito was put on the MI6's retainer contract so they could call on him anytime especially as he had shown he was more than just a pretty boy. Tito lived in two rooms not far from Victoria station so he found himself spending a lot of time in the more luxurious MI6 flat supplied to Shilpa.

"I can't stay on in London after September Tito. Jill says I should visit my father and his new wife. I don't know if I can face them. She is probably a gold-digger let's face it my father is no film star and he must be seventy one now and not a fit seventy one, at that, knowing him" she said cuddling up to him in bed.

"*Cara mia.* I only get a hundred pounds a month from the service as a retainer and then they will pay me for each job but I can't support you on that and I don't want you to live on the fifty they are giving you. Shilpa sorry but I have to go back to my old job as an escort and you won't like that. But while you are here I am only for you. *Credo di essere innamorato di lei,*" (*I think I am falling in love with you*) said Tito with tears in his eyes.

"You Italians are so soppy aren't you? I too love you but you are right it would never last and well this will be a happy memory for both of us," she kissed him on the cheek and then worked her way down his whole body till he was breathing heavily. They didn't sleep for the next two hours.

10
THE MEETING

The Air France flight landed in Nice on a sunny October morning. Shilpa took a cab to the small hotel she had booked over the Internet. The landlady was English and had moved there years ago when her husband retired and sold his business. This was more a hobby than a business to live on.

"Hello my dear Miss Moray. Had a good flight then? Lovely here isn't it? We love it here don't we Roland? Yes we do," she said in rapid succession not allowing Shilpa to reply to any of the questions.

After Shilpa had settled in she asked for the way to the Marina as Jill had even found out the name and berth of Ajit More's yacht. She walked the mile to the marina getting whistles from the men on a construction site. Well, she thought not bad for a 41-year-old chick. She admired the rows of super yachts and small floating palaces looking for Number 26. The marina is to the east below the Old Town of Cannes where lies the Vieux Port, or Old Port, also known as Port Cannes I. It's set inside the town so surrounded by buildings so the boats have a narrow channel to get to the sea.

After about twenty minutes strolling around she saw the Indian flag about five boats down so walked towards it to find it was number 26-'My Bombay Baby.' Trust Ajit More to call his yacht that. She walked the gangway and heard some voices on the top deck so made her way there to find six people playing cards. Her father was in a pair of trunks, no top but wearing a captain's cap.

"Hello can we help you young lady?" he said not really interested in her.

"Yes I think you can I am here to meet Ajit More (she said it correctly-Moray) is he around?" said Shilpa wondering when he would recognize her.

"That's me. Come join us always room for a pretty lady at my table."

"Thank you but I need to see you alone. It's been a long time."

Ajit got up and walked towards Shilpa and then suddenly stopped in his tracks.

"Oh my God is it really you?" his hands and body started to shake she realized immediately he must have Parkinson's disease but that just flashed through her mind.

Shilpa walked towards him slowly as the five people at the table sat speechless watching the drama unfold. Ajit shaking more and more couldn't move towards her so she took three quick steps forward and he grabbed her around the shoulder and started to weep. She just stood there with her arms by her side.

After about a minute of hearing him sob she lifted her arms and placed them lightly round his back and patted him gently. For a while the earth stood still for both of them and all she could feel was his aging body shaking against her and her, the right shoulder getting wet with his tears and saliva. He finally took a deep breath and looked at her again, kissed her on both cheeks and then turned around to the table and said "Friends this is my daughter. She was lost and now is found. Thank God Almighty!"

A woman who looked in her forties walked up to them and put her left arm around Ajit and with the right hand offered to shake Shilpa's hand but Shilpa ignored it.

"Welcome to our home from home. I am Shalini you must have heard of me I am sure," she said smugly.

Shilpa just nodded, looked around the deck to see the others nodding at her and some even said hello. Shalini asked if she wanted a drink but Shilpa just shook her head. One of the guests came up to them and gently put his arms around Shalini's shoulders saying, "She is in shock. I think you better let me see to her. They both need to be alone for a while. Can you get me a bottle of brandy and got any Valium?" Asked Dr. Lowell, from Boston, a retired heart surgeon now a Cannes summer resident.

He then went back to the father and daughter who were still just holding each other without saying a word. "Come with me you two. You both need a drink and need to be alone for a while," he said guiding them to the main cabin where they sat down and slowly sipped the brandy.

The party broke up and it was three hours later that Shalini came into the main cabin where Ajit and Shilpa had been talking to ask if they wanted to eat as it was 6 pm and some more people were coming.

"Cancel everything for the next two days and please don't disturb us," said Ajit abruptly.

"Darling we can't cancel now they will be here in thirty minutes. We have invited four people to dinner. "Shilpa can join us can't you?" She pleaded.

"Shalini you bloody mad or something. Do you have any idea what has just happened today? This is my daughter who I haven't seen in years and thought she was dead and you are going on about a bloody dinner! Take the lot out to dinner and the two of us will eat here, tell Jacobs to serve us here in a while. Just call him I will talk to him," he said really annoyed at Shalini's insensitivity.

Father and daughter spoke till 10 pm when she started to yawn he suggested she sleep in the guest cabin but she said she needed to get back and they would meet in the morning, as she knew where he was staying at the Hotel Cannes. Ajit called for Jacobs their butler-chef to take Shilpa back in a cab to her hotel. He then took him aside and put 500 Euros in his hand and told him to give it to Shilpa's landlady.

The following morning Shilpa joined her father and Shalini for breakfast at the Hotel Cannes. The couple had taken a suite for the summer, as Shalini didn't like to sleep on the boat when it was in dock but enjoyed flaunting her yacht to the friends and her relatives from India. Ajit had ordered breakfast in the room, which gave Shilpa a chance to see the place first hand.

What caught her eye immediately were the shoes in one closet, there must have been over thirty pairs of designer footwear, the likes of Jimmy Choo, Manolo Blahnik, Ferragamo and Bruno Magli to name a few. Her dresses came from London, Paris, Rome and LA: Gucci, Prada, Marc Jacobs and Versace. She recalled all her mother ever had were some good silk saris that must have cost half of what the Gucci dress cost.

Shalini was born to a Sindhi father one Rohit Shivdasani and an Anglo-Indian mother, Sandra 'Sandi' Farley who came from Calcutta and met Rohit in Bombay in the late 50s. She was a singer in restaurants in those days when hotels and eateries had small bands and singers who made their extra money singing at wedding and Parsee 'navjotes' (holy string ceremony).

Rohit was able to send his daughter Shalini to a finishing school in England but she was expelled for having an affair with the riding instructor. Fair skin and buxom she was able to get agents to get her bra modelling work because she had spent Saturday night, Sunday morning with them. Her main obsession was to make Bollywood films and her chance came when a production came to London and she was cast as "the foreign girlfriend" a bit part where she was on the screen for eight minutes. She had a fling with the young star who persuaded her to return to India with him. The only problem was he had his wife and two kids and so the affair had to stop, but in fairness to the actor he did get her a role in a serial, which was produced by Ajit More's Metro TV.

Ajit was known to quietly have his flings with young girls who were in his productions; Shalini happen to be one of them who he bedded every other week in a hotel room he kept in Bombay. Once he was condemned to prison no one wanted to know him even the young actresses who put up with him to advance their careers were disgusted and so when he came out of prison the only one that showed any loyalty was Shalini.

Ajit sold the TV station for forty-five million dollars some of which was paid under the table by a major corporation into a Swiss bank account. He revealed only thirty million and paid his wife five million for the divorce and another six million to the taxman, which he confessed to Shalini during a weak moment in bed one afternoon.

Shalini saw her chance and made herself indispensable to Ajit for his every need so within a year of the divorce they went on a Mediterranean cruise where the captain married them.

Seeing all the super yachts and palaces on the sea Shalini persuaded Ajit to buy a stunning, used, Sunseeker 90Y for two million dollars. She had four cabins and eight berths. He named her "My Bombay Baby" and she carried a compliment of three, captain, engineer and a sailor. Jacob was not part of the crew as he was considered Ajit's butler-chef and Man Friday.

Shalini had a couple of credit cards, which she spent like there was no tomorrow. An average shopping spree would be between ten and fifteen thousand dollars. She only gave to charity when there was a big dinner and she could be seen bidding for some art object or luxury vacation. Ajit was past caring as he was now a sick man with his Parkinson's and knew his days were numbered. He had been despondent when he heard about Shilpa escaping and not knowing where she was but time heals and it did that where she was concerned.

"Do you want me to buy you some clothes Shilpa?" Asked Shalini.

"No, I think I would like my father to buy me some clothes and whatever else I need, thank you," replied Shilpa.

"Here darling take this," said Ajit handing her a wad of notes. "I think there must be about two thousand there if you need more let me know." He went up to Shilpa and hugged her for over a minute and then said to Shalini "If she wants anything just charge it to the card and don't argue with her."

"Thank you daddy," said Shilpa and then turned to Shalini and said, "OK lets burn some paper in Cannes. I see from the collection in here you are an expert at burning money."

Shalini narrowed her eyes and thought I am going to show her who owns Ajit More and it's not his bloody daughter. "Ajit darling we will be off then," said kissing him on the lips. "We'll see you for lunch at the L'Affable on rue La Fountaine I hear it's got a divine new chef from Paris. Do you know it Shilpa?"

"You know I don't so don't ask silly bloody questions. Look I think I will go on my own and see you two at 1 pm for lunch at this "divine" café," said Shilpa then walked up to her daddy and kissed him before she stepped out.

"Watch it Shalini my girl is a tigress so do not awaken a sleeping tigress as you will find she is more ferocious than anything you can imagine. Treat her with respect after what she has been through and talking of respect treat my money with respect, these absurd shopping sprees need to stop. You are only showing off and don't need any of this stuff," said More as he paced around the room and then shaking he sat down.

Shilpa strolled down Rue d'Antibes, the main shopping street of Cannes she suddenly thought of the mountains of Afghanistan and the horrible conditions they lived in. She actually pinched her cheek to remind her this was real and she was there to blow a lot of money. Along the way she stopped to eat a crepe from the street cart smothered with Grand Marnier liqueur. She smiled at people who smiled back as if they all knew each other- with a Bonjour here and an hola there.

Finally she reached *Galerie marchande Gray d'Albion* the biggest shopping place in Cannes, filled with every type of chic and stylish boutique you could possibly imagine. Her eyes were swimming in the glitter that surrounded her and when she saw the prices her two thousand dollars seemed like petty cash. A Hermes scarf was fifteen hundred and a small Chanel dress was three thousand. She smiled and decided just to walk around when suddenly she stopped and stared.

There was Shalini arm in arm with a tall, grey haired man of about fifty. They were clearly not just friends as she was biting his hand playfully and he was kissing her forehead, as he was eight inches taller than her.

Well with not much to spend at these prices she followed the couple to see where they would go. First it was Hugo Boss, where Shalini came out with a large box, which had been paid for by the tall man as Shilpa had noticed.

They then stopped at Zara the Spanish shop and finally at the trendy boutique Paul & Shark. Laden with bags she stood at the entrance of the shop and kissed the man passionately. Shilpa wished she had a cell phone with a camera, she didn't even have a cell phone.

The street clock said 12.45 so she made her way back to the restaurant asking directions from a couple of people. On her arrival Ajit was already sitting at the table, which gave them a chance to talk but Ajit was upset Shilpa wasn't able to afford anything. "Don't worry after lunch you and I will go alone and you get what your heart desires," said Ajit with pride having his daughter sit next to him. They both ordered Mint Juleps and were actually laughing when Shalini walked in and said, "What's so funny?"

"Nothing you would understand. Why are you so late we have been here for twenty minutes?"

"Oh I was trying to get my nails done for tonight and the silly girl forgot my appointment. I will have to go after lunch, sorry," she said.

"No problem my daughter and I are going to make Cannes very rich this afternoon and your husband very poor, right darling? Oh, It's so good to have my baby back with me it's like a dream come true," sighed Ajit and leant over and kissed Shilpa on the cheek. "Ha, I see you have gone and made Cannes rich already. Why are you wasting so much of my hard earned money?" Cried out Ajit to Shalini.

Shalini didn't say a word to Shilpa all though lunch who dominated the conversation with daddy. Shalini hadn't heard Ajit laugh so much in years. What's she got I haven't got she thought to herself.

Shalini tried to add to the conversation by telling them about the food here;

"This is one of our favourite restaurants in Cannes is L'Affable, I love the modern décor and very good service. The food is always good and at lunchtime they do a very good deal for 23 euros for 2 courses or 27 for 3. Today had the dish of the day - guineafowl with tagliatelle and mushrooms and their signature dish of the grand Marnier...it's a must Shilpa, trust me you will love it," said Shalini gushing.

Well it can't be poison at this stage so why not and they all decided to have the guineafowl. Ajit hands started to shake a bit so Shalini gave him some meds.

"I must leave you two have to get my nails done. Bye." She was off. She was 'off' all right with the tall stranger. Shilpa walked fast for while asking daddy to wait and noted Shalini and the man walk up to a narrow house and then drew the curtains and switch on the window AC unit. The Bitch! She is screwing my dad every which way she can and I am going to stop it.

On her return to her dad she asked if he was really happy with Shalini.

"Well, *beti* at my age one has to be grateful for small mercies. When I came out of prison after they condemned me for dealing in arms and money laundering I was very lonely. Your mother asked for a divorce whilst I was in jail and you were gone so this woman was the only one who stood by me when I came out. I owe her that much and for a while I was happy but now with this Parkinson's and stomach problems I am not able to make her physically happy so I have to allow the nonsense that is going on," said Ajit feeling very despondent.

"You know about her affairs then?" asked Shilpa.

"Yes, yes what to do yar! What I resent is her spending my money on those bastards. They are like sponges just soaking her up and she loves it," sighed Ajit.

"What do I mean to you daddy?" she asked very sweetly.

"The whole world my darling. I was thinking just this morning I need to redo my will and put you in it now. I am so glad to see you in my life again. We must inform your mother she really did despair when you went missing."

Ajit pulled out his cell phone dialled a number in India. Shanta More and answered at the other end and just wept for several minutes on hearing Shilpa's voice.

"My daughter whatever they say about you I forgive you. There is so much to talk about but not now. I am so happy you are safe and with us again. Give me some time and we will talk for a long time," she said hanging up the receiver.

"This is all too surreal I can't believe this is happening to me daddy. I am so sorry for what I have done and I think God is giving me another chance," said Shilpa and fell into her father's shaking arms.

When Shalini returned Shilpa could swear she could smell "sex" on her, after all she knew the smell well. She had to get this woman out of her father's life and move back herself.

11
TITO RETURNS

That evening after they had been on a shopping spree and spent over ten thousand euros which included an Apple iPhone that had recently been introduced to the world. Her first call was to Tito in London to ask him to come down to Cannes and she would pay for the ticket. Two days later handsome and virile as ever Tito landed at Nice airport and Shilpa was there in her rented Porsche to pick him up.

They made a very good-looking couple in the perfect setting of the Riviera. She drove the car along the Cornish and up to Grasse so they could have an undisturbed day and night together. They booked into a hotel that was once a perfume garden where roses and other flowers were plucked and dried for scents. Most of those places have gone now and it's all chemistry in Swiss labs.

The four-poster bed had a mirror on top that allowed the lovers to watch their performance for most of the night. Finally after 2 am Shilpa went to sleep weary and dripping in sweat which Tito licked like he was enjoying the last of a dessert plate.

She allowed Tito to drive the Porsche back to Cannes and straight to the yacht where a group of people were playing cards on the deck. This time Ajit proudly presented his daughter to all the guests and then welcomed Tito as the man who saved his daughter in Afghanistan.

Shalini didn't miss the touch of Tito's hands. He was younger than her usual lovers and a hunk to add to it. Tito didn't miss the extra squeeze from her either. Their eyes met and a message was passed. Tito was a master with older women. The other person who didn't miss the meeting was Shilpa and she smiled to herself.

A couple of days earlier before Tito arrived Shilpa had moved on to the yacht and taken over the second bedroom. She invited Tito to stay there with her and told the crew this was going to be their home for the next few weeks. She got the captain to take them out to sea and sailed around the coast to Spain and then to Gibraltar and finally back to Cannes. It was the first real holiday she had had in years and Tito was the perfect companion.

"Tito my love I want you to do me a special favour, will you?" she calmly asked him on the deck as they sailed into the marina.

"For you anything. These past seven days have been something very special to me and I thank you so much. When I go with the others there is no real love or passion it's just my business I have to act all the time but this time I wanted you and missed you in London so much and was so happy when you called. Yes, what you want me to do?" He said, kissing her hard on the lips and then held her in his arms, he was falling in love.

"I want you to seduce Shalini she is milking my father and I want to get her out of his life. I need to get my father back and do something worthwhile with my life. You have already guessed he is very rich now and this bitch is taking him for all he has and I want to find a way to stop it. If you seduce her and for a while it will have to look like I am really angry at you but then my father may have a change of heart and divorce her,' said Shilpa.

"Are you serious? I can't do that to you and sleep with your stepmother. Even I have some scruples Shilpa. What are you thinking? She can have any man around your boat, they all look at her with lust in their eyes," said Tito so indignant.

"You are special to me Tito so I can say this to you and know you will not feel anything for that vampire. Please think about it. We have the rest of our lives together and you won't need to work again like you do," said Shilpa.

They didn't say another word to each other until the ship docked and they heard a cry of welcome from Ajit and Shalini who were waving to them from the landing.

"You sure you know what you are asking me to do?" asked Tito. Shilpa nodded yes.

Tito was the first off the yacht and shook hands with Ajit and thanked him for a wonderful trip then saw Shalini's face and hugged her like an old friend and in the process lightly kissed her on the lips while squeezing her hand slowly.

Shilpa followed and hugged her daddy for a full minute then touched cheeks with Shalini.

A car was waiting for them to be whisked off to a place that was to be a surprise. The chauffeur drove the large Mercedes to a destination only known to Ajit even Shalini was in the dark. Situated on a hillside, just a hop from Saint-Tropez's centre and Pampelonne beaches, Château de la Messardière spans the Bay of Saint-Tropez, vineyards of Ramatuelle and the Med. Built in the 19th century and fully restored. The 5-star Château de la Messardière—regarded as a genuine institution in Saint-Tropez—has maintained all its extraordinary original character. Shilpa and Tito were overwhelmed as they drove at the pink and white arches and flooring of the entrance.

"What is this?" asked Shilpa.

"Somewhere my daughter can really relax and find her old self again. It has everything you need to pamper your mind and body for the next week and then we will see what we are going to do. So my children and wife this is your playground for the next six nights, enjoy," said Ajit feeling very satisfied with himself as he looked at the "gob-smacked" faces of his party.

The first day was typical of a spa; massages, hair oiled, manicures and pedicures and eating delicious light meals and drinking fruit and vegetable juices. On the next day after the morning routine Shilpa took Tito to the pool, which overlooked the ocean and asked him if he was prepared to do what she requested of him regarding Shalini.

"Are you sure this is what you want and if I do what will we get out of it? He asked.

"I want my father to catch you both," said Shilpa.

"What are you crazy?"

"No I will convince my daddy that it was her and not you and that we are still together but I want him to really feel hurt so he will get rid of her."

Tito found this all too bizarre and shook his head and walked back into the hotel. As he was walking through the glass doors he bumped into Shalini looking very fetching in her swimsuit, just then his heart skipped a beat as he had never thought of her in a sexual way before but now she was very appealing. I must be mad he said to himself but then took Shalini's hand and said "Come on let's have a race in the pool I will give you a start."

She didn't say a word but kept hold of his hand and they both jumped into the pool and started to laugh. Shilpa seeing this exited the area quickly as she knew Tito had a change of mind.

Shalini and Tito frolicked in the pool and swam silly races for almost half an hour then he suggested they take a walk on the beach. Hand in hand they walked not saying much except talking about the weather, food and the yacht but the hands stayed tightly clasped. They arrived at a spot where Tito thought they were out of range from the hotel so he stopped turned her around and kissed her on the lips. She in turn threw her arms around his neck and opened his mouth with her tongue. Tito forced her to the sand and she unzipped her swimsuit from the front exposing her body. He in turn pushed down his trunks and without any foreplay entered Shalini who gave out a loud holler as he thrust himself into her.

"Don't stop, harder, faster. Oh my God. I am coming. Ahhh!" She came and then within ten seconds so did he but then didn't roll over as so many men do instead started to kiss her breasts, thighs and legs. Shalini had not had sex like this in years. She took his head and kissed him all over his face. "What are we going to do? I can't get enough of you," she said. Tito smiled and said nothing just laid back in the sand letting the sun tan his whole body.

Back in the dining room Ajit and Shilpa were enjoying their diet meal of water chestnut soup and fruit salad with slivers of grilled duck. "So where are those two?" asked Ajit.

"God knows and who cares. I want to have some time with you now. I still have dreams and nightmares about Afghanistan. They say it will be a long time before I am rid of these memories, if ever. Last night I woke Tito up because I dreamt I was being raped by those bastards," she said and started to cry.

"You are here with me now and you don't have to go anywhere. I need you more than you need me *beti* believe me. For all I know that wife of mine is seducing your boyfriend right now," he said.

That evening Tito came into the bedroom to find Shilpa having a head massage by a spa assistant. She had her hair oiled and a towel wrapped around her. "Where have you been all day? Daddy and I were worried," she said.

"Doing what you asked me to do. I must be mad," he said going into the bathroom.

Shilpa smiled and couldn't wait to ask him what happened so she dismissed the girl and walked into the shower with Tito. She pressed up against him and said, "Tell me all and do not leave out the details."

So with the two 'rain showers' covering them he went into the details and that turned them both on and before he had even finished they were on the floor of the shower cabin making love so intensely that Tito was covered with the almond oil from Shilpa's hair.

"What's the plan you two have hatched for tomorrow?" she asked as they were drying each other with seven-foot long Turkish towels with the hotel crest.

"You really want me to go on with this?"

"Why didn't you enjoy it?"

"Actually she is amazing but not as amazing as you, really. I never met Indian women before and my friend always said they were very shy and not full of action but you two are awesome. Is that the right word?"

"Well don't get too carried away with her she is the enemy you know."

The next day Shilpa and Ajit planned to go for a drive, Shalini faked a bad stomach and Tito wanted to relax by the pool and work on his tan. So the father daughter duo went off with the car to see the villages on the top of the hills.

Tito convinced Shalini it was safe to come to his room and spend the afternoon there. After a very wild session they ordered room service to bring tea and cakes and then slept soundly for the next hour.

The clock in the lobby struck five as Ajit and Shilpa returned. As she suspected something she asked Ajit to her room to find two naked bodies on the bed fast asleep.

"This is the thanks I get for bringing you here Mr. Tito you shameless pig," yelled Ajit and walked over with his arms raised to hit him. Tito, the stronger man, got hold of his arms and pushed them down saying, "Let me explain it's not like you think.."

"What can I think?"

"You lousy son of a bitch you do this to me!' yelled Shilpa and then Shalini started to cover herself and shouted out, "Stop this all of you. I need some love in my life. How long can a woman be without some physical attention? You can't give it to me so I have to find it where I can and he is wonderful. You Shilpa should appreciate him more and not ignore him like you have done."

Shilpa ran across the room and slammed her fists into Shalini who tried to fight back but was at a disadvantage being on the bed and naked. Ajit walked up to Tito who was covering his privates with a pillow and slapped him but in respect to the senior man Tito took it and just stared at Shilpa who was still screaming at Shalini. The ruckus caused the hotel security to come in to the room, which was still open and saw the riot going on. One of the security men ran into the bathroom and brought out a robe and placed it over Shalini and asked Tito to cover himself properly.

"We will have to make a report of this to the manager," said one of the security guards.

"Please don't do that," said Ajit. "I will make it worth your while, please give me a few minutes and come to my suite and talk to me."

The two men looked at each other and nodded and then making a sign with his hands the senior one implied now calm down and no more noise.

Ten minutes later there was a knock on Ajit's door, which Shalini, now back in her room, opened to see the two guards standing there. She invited them in and offered them a drink which at first they refused but then after she poured out two glasses of 2005 Château Mont-Redon, Côtes-du-Rhône Rouge which they both knew cost a fortune, in fact about 75 Euros, they could hardly say no and any way they were there to get a 'tip.'

Ajit More walked out of the bathroom still very angry and held out two hundred Euro notes and thanked both men for their discretion. The two men downed the wine that should have been sipped and left the room.

Ajit then turned to Shalini and said, "I think it's time you and I had a separation. I have known your goings on for three years now but this was the last straw and that with my daughter's man. Yes I know he is a gigolo but did you have to prove it to me and for what?"

Shalini said nothing but went to the bed and lay face down on the pillow crying.

"Shalini, I was telling Shilpa how you stood by me when I came out of prison but I don't think you ever loved me as such. You loved my millions so now dear girl I am going to give you some of it and ask you to get out of my life. I am going to sleep in the living room tonight and I want you to arrange for a car to take you back to Cannes in the morning and then to where ever you want to go but I don't want to see you for a while," said Ajit very calmly and walked out of the suite to Shilpa's suite.

The door was still ajar and so Ajit knocked slowly pushing it open to find Tito and Shilpa in an embrace.

"Have you made up so soon? I just told Shalini to leave me and be out of here in the morning. I would have said right now but I don't want to make a scene downstairs. But what's going on here?"

Shilpa looked sheepish and Tito looked like he was caught with his hands in the cookie jar.

"Yes as I thought it was Shalini who was blackmailing him. I have to tell you that Tito works for the MI6 in London and if they knew he was here with me he would be in serious trouble and so he was just doing her bidding," lied Shilpa.

"Yes sir, she is correct that is what happened. Shilpa and I worked in Afghanistan together it's a part of her life that she hasn't told you about," said Tito.

"Well I have all the time in the world now so start to tell me about MI6 if that is really true," said Ajit sitting down on a sofa. Shilpa poured him a drink and then she and Tito told him all about their time with MI6.

12
HOW WHAT

Ajit More couldn't sleep a wink the night he heard Shilpa and Tito's story about the service in the British Secret Intelligence Service or MI6. It was so strange that he was sure she could never make up such a lie, not even his devious daughter.

He opened his Bhagavad-Gita and started to read it and read the words aloud to himself. After all the wrong he had done in his life like the arms deals with Ashok Kapoor and the money laundering and cheating with younger women he needed to make amends with his god and himself.

That morning at breakfast he invited both Tito and Shilpa to join him in a trip. They took the rented Bentley and had the driver take them to La Lumière a divine haven in the hills of the Provence.

"It's a temple of nature," said Ajit "Here the plan is to get in touch with yourself. They offer you this quiet place to find sanctuary during your stay, and to take time for your spiritual growth." As they drove up the snake road the Mediterranean disappeared from view.

"What I want us to do is to participate in daily spiritual discipline of ashram living, morning and evening meditations and rituals. Receive individual spiritual guidance to evoke God within us. You both will love the sensual setting of Provence; we honor all religions, and celebrate the Spirit of Love. Meditate, chant in ceremony, harvest lavender, pluck figs and olives. All of us need to return to our center and find harmony by remembering the presence of your true natural self," said Ajit in a very somber tone.

Shilpa wondered if he was all right or had the dismissal of Shalini affected him mentally. She thought Tito and me in a damn ashram he has to be kidding! Well whatever and so they drove for the next several hours till they reached La Lumiere where an attractive lady in her forties greeted them by quoting a Chinese proverb; 'A house only becomes a home if your body finds strength, your mind rest and your soul peace.' Welcome to your new home. Let me show you to your rooms."

They walked in the sunshine smelling the freshly cutgrass, the breeze was soft and the faint aroma of the eucalyptus trees had a calming effect on the three new comers. Tito was the first to react aloud and say, "You know I think this might work for us."

He took Shilpa's hand and put his arms around Ajit's shoulders as they walked through the grounds to their cabins.

Catherine, the guide, turned to them and said, "There is no must, a lot of space for joy, for giggles, for laughter and for a lot of food. It's like a huge storage space for my happiness. This pool that one can dive into again and again contains something life changing for me. Because the feeling I carry within me is expressed in a real place and it is good to know that one can refill one's energy here. Light-heartedness, joy at work and self-discovery are all permitted here. At home, I inject this into my work and art." Catherine was a TV producer from the mid-west and had been through a bad marriage. A friend suggested she come to France and she had been here for over six months considering she came for only two weeks.

The days went by quickly and the stress began to fall off slowly. The hardest part was meditation as the mind never rested even with the "guru" calling for deep breaths and "let it all go." Then on the fifth day when the session was over they noticed Tito still sitting here and slowly swaying but in another zone. The guru signaled to Shilpa and Ajit to get up quietly and leave the room to Tito, which they did.

"Daddy, I can't believe he has found 'It,' hasn't he? Said Shilpa. Ajit nodded and smiled.

As the days went by Tito became very remote, he would wander off on his own into the woods or walk around the spectacular lake with the hills reflecting in its glass like surface. Shilpa felt relaxed but found meditation difficult and still woke up at nights with nightmares. Ajit on the other hand went and asked the Durga, who is the head person, to anoint him. So he had to prepare:

"Mix the red and yellow shandam powder each with rose water. A bowl with sugar water (one part sugar, one part water) and some drops of jasmine oil and energize it with "Om Amrith Jay" for this you need an initiation from Durga. Decorate the fire place. Mix the red and yellow shandam powder each with rose water. Once this is done then you bow to the 8 wind directions (4 directions of the compass and the 4 cosmic winds and chant "Om Mahashakti Jay" for each direction, starting east. Then put the bowl with sugar water in the middle of the woodpile and spread the camphor for lighting under the wood. Light the fire and sing 3 times Om Namah Shivaya," said the Durga.

Once they had all chanted and hugged each other Ajit took Shilpa aside and said "Daughter I need to confess something to you."

They walked away from the campfire and sat on a log looking at the stars in silence. After about two minutes Ajit said, "You are my daughter and always have been but not my biological child."

"What do you mean? Am I adopted?"

"Yes, just listen please and then ask questions if you must. My late brother, your uncle Rajesh, was your real father and he had an affair with the maid who you were born to. We had suggested an abortion but she really loved Rajesh and chose to have his child so we sent her to live in a guest house in Panchgani which is a hill station about two hundred miles from Bombay. Your mother and I went on a European holiday and cruise with the promise to her and my brother we would adopt the child. When we heard she had given birth we returned and went straight to Panchgani and collected you. We made sure that the woman, her name was Bharati, was compensated well and we told the world you were our baby. We have never had adoption papers for you. Your real mother's wish was that you be called Shilpa after her mother so we agreed. If you are to ask where is she now I have no idea. It's been over forty years my baby."

Shilpa sat stunned and just stared at the stars. The sky was like black velvet sprinkled with white rice.

Tito walked over and gave Ajit a 'Namaste" greeting with folded palms and congratulated him on his anointment.

"Why are you both so sad?" he asked.

"Oh, something we should have talked about thirty years ago. I need to be alone for a while Tito," said Shilpa.

Ajit got up and took Tito's arm and walked him back to the campfire.

At the end of two weeks all three decided it was time to return to Cannes and then decide what to do next. The trip had calmed them all down and each one had lost some weight so looked a lot healthier. What was important now was what's next?

13
RETURN TO BASE

RETURN TO BASE AT ONCE. YOUR LITTLE DALIANCE IS OVER AND IT'S TIME TO GO TO WORK. REPORT AT ONCE TO THE OFFICE ON MONDAY, 9 SHARP. (THERE WAS NO SIGNATURE).

Tito stared at the cable for several seconds and then realised his life wasn't his own anymore and that they had known where he and Shilpa were every second since he left London over one month ago. Damn them but it did give him a job he was secretly proud of serving his adopted country.

"Do you really have to go? Asked Shilpa.

"Yes and they really must need me otherwise they wouldn't have put up with my going away for so long. I must go; it's been the best part of my entire life. I won't forget you *mia caro*," said Tito and kissed her gently.

Three hours later she left Tito at Nice airport and returned to her father at the yacht only to find Shalini waiting on the deck in her swim togs and sunglasses.

"You bitch you didn't think you could get rid of me so fast did you? Asked Shalini

"Don't you ever call me a bitch again," said Shilpa and smacked Shalini on the face that sent her against the deck rails and then went for her again and hit her with her right fist and pushed her into the water.

The two sailors of the crew saw the action from a distance and came running out. They threw Shalini a life buoy and tried to haul her in on a rope. Then one of them dived into the shallow water and hoisted her up with the help of the other sailor at the end of the rope.

Shalini was in shock and Shilpa went up to her and hit her again at which point the captain came and told her to stop it and called her father to come up.

Ajit was surprised to hear the story but more so to see Shalini there all wet and fuming.

"Leave us," said Ajit. "You too Shilpa go to your cabin I need to speak to Shalini alone."

"Listen you, I have had enough of you and your nonsense. I want you to take your stuff in the next hour, get Jacob to help and get off my ship. I will contact you in time. Send me a post card as to where you are and do not spend more than $5,000 in the next month, as I will be giving orders to American Express that is your limit. Now go and I don't want to see you again. We will talk through our lawyers," said Ajit and walked back to his cabin.

October is a lovely time on the Riviera, it not hot and yet one can swim and take in the air on the deck without feeling chilly. The sun was a large orange setting in the west with an afterglow of pink, then red then purple. Father and daughter sipped Cinzanos and marvelled at nature. They asked the captain and crew to join them, which was rare, and Jacob made some superb canapés and roasted quails for a snack. The conversation subjects changed to sea stories thanks to the sailors and the captain. They even asked Shilpa if the rumours about her Afghan days were true. She made it into a joke and they laughed into the night having gone through 4 bottles of *Veuve Clicquot* at $70 per bottle. The captain was the first to say 'Good night' and then the others followed soon after leaving the father and daughter alone. It was only 10 pm.

Shilpa thought of Tito and what he was up to. Ajit in turn was thinking of his daughter and wondering what she was up to. A tigress doesn't change her stripes he thought although he was glad to have got rid of Shalini.

"What do you want to do now? Asked Ajit.

"I think I want to go to America as I can't go back to India till the MI6 gives me a clearance and I think they will in a year or so. Do you remember Darius Cooper? Well I want to find him. I believe he is in San Diego, California. Yes I think I want to find him," she said in a pondering tone.

"Do you think he even remembers you? And any way he may be married now," said Ajit.

"Oh he is married I know that but just want to surprise him. I think he really liked me under all that anger and disapproval of his. Yes, I want to find him now,"

"Don't go ruining a good marriage daughter. Let sleeping dogs lay, its best. You can't go back you know. This Tito seems like a nice man lets cultivate him and make him into a partner in a business you and I can do. Think of something, we can afford to go into any business we like and you have a future and Tito can be your right arm and lover and may be husband," said Ajit.

"I do fear if I leave you that bitch will be back as you will be lonely and take her back for companionship or whatever. Know what I mean."

"I wish my health was better I would like a eighteen year old nymph to keep me happy at nights but sadly I can't do much now. All this money and no can do body. Well its God's punishment to me and I have to thank my stars it's not worse."

"Dad I want to go to the USA. I have a ticket from the firm and so let me go for a month or so. You will be OK won't you? Please don't entertain that cow, please!"

⸺✦⊱✦⊰✦⸺

Three days later Shilpa was at De Gaulle airport in Paris on her Air France flight to New York and then Delta to San Diego after spending a few days in the Big Apple.

Two days after her arrival in New York she had a brain wave-call Mac and Molly and see if they recall her. She dialed the New Jersey police and asked where she could find those two. It took a while, as Mac who was now Captain Ian McGregor and Molly Shaft was Detective Sergeant first class, she was bucking for a lieutenant's post.

When she finally got Mac on the line he was dumbstruck without saying a word to Shilpa he called out to Molly who came running thinking someone had been murdered in the office.

"You are not going to believe who this is on this line," said McGregor.

"Who for Christ sake?"

"Guess? A blast from the past, I'll say no more." He hit the 'more'

"You don't say. Shilpa Moray! AHH! You are kidding aren't you?"

He handed her the phone and cautiously Molly said "Hello Shilpa."

"Hello Molly. It's really me I am here in New York can we please meet up I have so much to tell you. It's all so surreal," said Shilpa.

"Where are you?"

"I am staying at the Lexington on East 48th and Lexington Avenue can you meet me there?"

Molly looked at Mac and he nodded and within an hour the three were hugging each other in the lobby of the hotel.

They went up to her room and opened a bottle of Champagne that the New Jersey police had brought with them to celebrate. Shilpa ordered some snacks and they sat and discussed their lives for the next two hour.

"We lost you in the Khyber Pass as you must have left your shoes and bag in different places and the signal is not good there. We really thought you may have got out with Salim but when we caught up to him he told us the Taliban had taken you. By the way that scum is doing twenty years in a Federal prison.

We owe you a lot Shilpa and I was saying to Molly coming up we have to make it good for you now," said Mac.

Molly just kept staring at her and then said "There is a change in you. What did those people do to you?

Shilpa went into her horror stories and then about the British rescue and confessed to the surgery but not the MI6. She found her rich dad he was fine, about the awful wife and made them laugh about how she got rid of her- same old Shilpa thought the cops.

"We need to do something for you. You went way past what you had to do for us. Will you allow me to get in touch with the CIA again and see how we can compensate you? Asked Mac.

"Sure why not. I am looking for something to do," she said.

The room meeting went into an early dinner at the Chinese Dynasty, in the hotel, one of the best of its kind in NYC. They then discussed what had happened in the past and would Shilpa with her experience like to talk to the CIA regarding a post even as a consultant. Mac had friends at CNC, Cable News Corporation, who would put her on the air as the specialist on Afghan affairs. Sure she would love it.

"Well let's see what I can do," said Mac and Molly said she wanted a girls night out with her soon.

Two days later Molly called to say the Director, no less, of the CIA wanted to meet Shilpa in person and they were sending a jet down to LaGuardia to fly her and Mac to Langley, Virginia. Just forty minutes after takeoff they landed at the special airfield for the CIA and a car rushed them to the massive halls of the building of the Central Intelligence Agency.

The Director was at a White House briefing so the Deputy Director (DD) stood in and greeted both Shilpa and Mac. After some pleasantries he asked to be left alone with Shilpa.

"Well you have certainly been through more than we imagined. I assume you haven't said a word to your cop out there about your MI6 experience," said the DD. Shilpa was shocked he knew about that. "The cousins and us share a lot of info these days after 9/11. Makes sense and after all we are fighting together out there and in Iraq."

"How much do you know?"

"Just about everything. Tito and all if you get my drift," he said smiling. "I am glad you found your father and now we will clear the way for you to meet your mother in India. In the mean time I understand you want to be kept busy so we have an idea... No not sending you back but much more glamorous.

We want you to join CNC, the news station, and be their Afghanistan expert and in the process get us info we need. How does that strike you? We will keep the MI6 between a few others and us. I want you to meet someone. Let's go and take our policeman with us.

Shilpa was thinking this is all a dream all over again. Oh My God!

Mac joined them as they went to the next floor and then into a room full of TV screens and gadgets that boggled Shilpa's mind. "Hey Diane come and meet the prodigal daughter," said the DD.

Diane Kruger, a lady in her fifties, walked over and hugged Shilpa. "Oh lord I can't tell you how happy I am to see you alive and well. You have no idea what we went through here on the day we lost you," she kissed Shilpa on both cheeks and held her face in her hands as if she was her own daughter. Mac then explained that Diane was the one in charge of tracking her into the pass.

They all went into the executive dining room for lunch and there the Director joined them and asked Shilpa formally if she would like to work for them in a special capacity and that the DD would fill her in. He already had done that and Shilpa happily accepted her new role as a TV personality and consultant to CNC.

14
A TIGRESS NEVER LOSES HER STRIPES

La Jolla is a suburb of San Diego once described as the best city in the USA. By the early years of the 21ˢᵗ century, 2006, it was enveloped in debt mainly by over spending in its heydays and the baby boomers beginning to retire with massive pension benefits. Lower taxes and a loss in employment were beginning to hinder the cities coffer.

Darius Cooper applied to several of the local universities but was told he needed a Master's degree to teach even when he said he had forty years of real practical experience the idiots at the school turned him down. Finally the local city college gave him a post of lecturer in Films and Television department. He also made local commercials and worked with the symphony to create new events for fund raising. All this gave him a livable income.

In turn Dalia kept her teaching job which helped pay for the bills. Theirs was a happy and calm existence till the day there was a knock on their door.

"Hello," said Dalia to the woman standing at her door in a Versace dress and high heels making her taller than her normal 5'-7."

"Hello, how are you?" asked the woman at the door.

"Fine thanks, can I help you?"

"Hi, Dalia I came to see you and Darius," said the woman.

Dalia stared and thought who the hell is this?

"Sorry but do we know you?" Asked a puzzled Dalia.

"It's been a long time. I am Shilpa," said Shilpa.

"Jesus Christ! Darius come here now, quickly," yelled Dalia and just stood staring at Shilpa.

"What's the matter? Hello, what's the problem?" Asked Darius.

"Don't you see who she is?" Asked Dalia while Shilpa stayed still as a statue.

Darius shook his head to say No.

"Think back Darry…" said Shilpa

"My God! How the bloody hell did you get here?" Asked Darius. "The tigress is back!"

"It wasn't easy to find you both," said Shilpa smiling at Darius' remark about the tigress.

"Well come in and sit please. Like something to drink? I could do with a brandy."

Yes, thought Shilpa–the tigress has returned!

Dalia went into the kitchen and brewed some coffee and brought it out but in all that time Darius and Shilpa had not said a word to each other. The Coopers were in a state of shock to say the least.

For the next hour Shilpa told them her story MI6 and all, after she finished Darius and Dalia Cooper were still non pas que. Dalia broke the silence by asking

"Where are you staying?"

"At the La Jolla Inn, sweet little place. You live in a gorgeous part of the world."

"Yes we do, we consider ourselves very lucky," said Darius.

Another long silence proceeded.

"It's almost dinner time would you like to share a meal with us?" Asked Dalia.

"That would be very kind, thank you."

Slowly Darius told his story and how worried they were about Shilpa and so on till he got to meeting Dalia again, she in her fifties and he in his sixties decided to marry and settle down in what the airlines like to call …"we are now landing in Paradise, I mean San Diego."

Dalia's stomach was churning but she served a lovely meal of lamb chops, peas and mash potatoes, followed by Hagen-Das coffee ice cream. It was almost 10 pm when they finished exchanging stories and Shilpa yawned, it was time to go.

"I will walk you back," said Darius.

"I too can do with a walk," said Dalia. Shilpa didn't miss that quick response knowing she would never trust Shilpa with her husband.

When the Coopers were returning home Dalia asked, "What does she want with us or better still with you"?

"God knows that woman may have changed but tigresses do not lose their stripes. Have to confess I had a soft spot for her but now I didn't even recognize her with the surgery and all that. It's been eight years. We lost her in 1998, wow how time flies," sighed Darius. Neither of them slept easily that night and the morning was even worse when Shilpa turned up with coffee and donuts from Dunkin' Donuts.

"Wake up you sleepyheads I have an offer to make to you guys and one that could make you rich, well better off. I can see you are just getting by now let me show you a way to get a bit richer in a short time and it will be legal," said bright and breezy Shilpa.

"I have been made a special correspondence to CNC to deal with the Taliban and Jihadists and I think the 3 of us can make a team. I have the OK for that. You Darry will be the producer. I need someone of your experience, Dalia you will be an associate producer and researcher, a lot better fun that teaching spotty deaf kids and I will be the face of CNC. Sorry you actually do a great service with those kids."

She continued, "There is a terrific story we can get on to right away. You two take a leave of absence and see if we can work together. This is going to be a big deal as I feel Syria is setting up for a civil war in a year or two. They are fed up with Assad and want to get him out so let's see how they are planning the revolution.

I also got this off the Internet it's a terrific story and no one has tumbled on it." She showed them the print out:

Tunisian Girls Are Coming Home Pregnant After Performing 'Sexual Jihad' In Syria

A number of girls from Tunisia have become pregnant after traveling to Syria to participate in "sexual jihad," according to Lotfi Bin Jeddo, Tunisia's Interior Minister.

The girls are (sexually) swapped between 20, 30, and 100 rebels and they come back bearing the fruit of sexual contacts in the name of sexual jihad and we are silent doing nothing and standing idle," Al Arabiya reported he said during an address to the National Constituent Assembly.

"After the sexual liaisons they have there in the name of 'jihad al-nikah' - (sexual holy war, in Arabic) - they come home pregnant," Ben Jeddou told the MPs.

He did not elaborate on how many Tunisian women had returned to the country pregnant with the children of jihadist fighters.

Jihad al-nikah**, permitting extramarital sexual relations with multiple partners, is considered by some hardline Sunni Muslim Salafists **as a legitimate form of holy war.

Jeddo also said his ministry had taken a number of steps to stem the flow of Tunisians travelling to Syria.

Tunisia's former Mufti (the country's highest religious official) warned earlier this year that 13 Tunisian girls "were fooled" into travelling to Syria to offer sexual services for the rebels. He described the practice as a form of "prostitution."

"For Jihad in Syria, they are now pushing girls to go there. 13 young girls have been sent for sexual jihad. What is this?" Battikh said.

Darius looked at Dalia and one could see his adrenaline pumping to get back into the field and do a risky story. "I have to talk it over, don't we Dalia?" asked Darius.

"What's it paying? Asked Dalia"

"About $1,500 for you and 2,500 a week for Darius. I get 3000 in case you have to know. The contract is for a year and then we see how things go. I know I have no journalist experience but the school of hard knocks has given me a doctorate in this field. Oh and all expenses of course."

"Give us till the morning," said Darius and they parted. Shilpa took the car and drove over to the Midway aircraft carrier in the city harbour which is now a museum of immense size; it takes 3 hours to get around it.

In La Jolla 'the 2 Ds,' as Shilpa now thought of them, sat and looked at each other.

"You really want this don't you? Asked Dalia

"Yep I really do, fed up with talking about the old days need something new."

"OK let's do it but keep your pecker in your pants as far as she is concerned or I will really cut it off and you won't find it!"

He didn't smile knowing she was serious.

Two days later they were on a flight to Langley and then to CNC in Atlanta to meet the bosses there where both Darius and Shilpa made the pitch and were given the green light to fly out as soon as they were ready. The green light actually took 2 full days as they went into the clearance procedure for both the CIA and CNC which, cleared all three of them.

In Atlanta the CNC HQ lies in midtown a long way from the 1990s when it started at a small converted warehouse with just $25,000,000. Darius recalled the friends he had in those days that worked there for small salaries.

Darius who was more experienced in these matters did the pitching of the story. They needed a cameraman who was willing to risk his life and equipment to satellite the stories back to HQ.

As often happens these production meetings went on forever, so it seemed to the inexperienced Shilpa and Dalia whereas Darius took them in his stride: who were their contacts, what all did they know about the place, how long did they anticipate being out there, what was the cost etc. The managers many of whom had never seen a foreign location were the most vocal as they always are.

The VP who was a former correspondent was less concerned and realised the experience of Darius but had concerns about Dalia and even more about Shilpa but he was also the only one who knew they all had CIA clearance.

They had started on Wednesday and now it was Sunday afternoon with lunch being served in the boardroom.

"Well I think we can leave the preproduction to Mr Cooper and give him all the help he needs. Get Tony Mane to be their tech op he is a good man and will take care of the entire technical side. OK then we have a Go on this. Good luck," said the VP and shook hands with the new crew before he left.

Tony Mane was an English man from the north of England. Still had the Yorkshire accent, which pleased Darius as it recalled school and BBC days of old. Tony had been to art school in Leicester and joined BBC news as a cameraman in the 60s but their paths had never crossed, as the departments were very separate. The BBC News ran from the news tower at TV Centre in White City where it had its own labs, cutting rooms and crews. They had nothing to do with the Film Unit in Ealing that did everything else and Darius worked with them in his capacity as Associate producer for 'Music and Arts.'

Shilpa threw herself into the task of talking to reporters, watching the anchors every time she had a chance and feeling confident she was in safe hands with Darius.

Dalia was the biggest surprise; in no time she mastered the computer and the media websites but in three days, with the help of some interns, had so much info on the story that even the VP was amazed. He said to Dalia, "Once this gig is over you have a job here if you want it."

They decided to first go to a friendly nation and say they were doing puff pieces on the growth of Casablanca with reference to the classic film with Bogart and Bergman. Needless to say it was Darius' idea. He wished there really had been Rick's American Café. The crew of Darius, Shilpa, Dalia and Tony flew into Casablanca.

They decided to film in the city, as it was one of the more liberal Islamic countries of the world and where the king still had a say. Darius and the crew sat up all night writing Shilpa's first voice over and her pieces to camera. It was important to open with her on camera, as this was her first report and people needed to see her perform.

There was no doubt the extremist and the Taliban were going to take notice of it and not only them but also the Iranians.

Shilpa took about four takes to get it right but when she did she looked like a natural.

"We are here in Casablanca as we thought this would be the safest place to launch our investigation into the slave trade of the Jihadists. To measure Islamic fundamentalists' success in controlling society is the depth and totality with which they suppress the freedom and rights of women. Since the overthrow of the Shah, the ruling mullahs have enforced humiliating and sadistic rules and punishments on women and girls. Forcing them to be segregated, wearing head gear, lashings for simply what the authorities call flirting and reducing them to second-class citizens but worst of all stoning them to death for their so called crimes," said Shilpa.

It was a lot to remember so Darius broke it up into segments and Tony shot it in close-ups and midshots that were edited later. Everyone gave Shilpa a round of applause as she finished her piece.

"Don't expect this every time," said Tony. "You are a pro now and we expect this and better from now on. Well done luv." He patted her on the shoulder.

The rest of the piece was narrated over library footage and interviews with women in the city. She got her information from people around and from the Internet. Her narrative was:

"Many people in this country do not realize that the Iranian government is involved in the trade of young women who come mainly from impoverished areas but are pretty and fair skinned. The colour of the skin is very important in this part of the world where most people tend to be dark or as some say café au lait.

The girls range from 15 to 29 and often have drug habits but the demand is great especially in the gulf countries and even in Europe. There is a confirmed report where a 16 year old was sold to a 58 year old European man in Turkey."

"Hundreds of girls between 12 and 18 are sold to men in Pakistan and then they are made to work in their homes as 'junior wives' or put to work in brothels. In the southeastern border province of Sistan Baluchestan, thousands of Iranian girls reportedly have been sold to Afghani men, where they wind up no one seems to know. In this series we are going to investigate this trade and no doubt will upset a lot of people. The only thing that will stop this is the end of rule by these tyrants in these countries who abuse the Koran and it's teaching. In Casablanca this is Shilpa Moray, CNC." Shilpa signed off her first report.

Two days later it aired on CNC International and CNC at home and there was an outcry that they never expected. The Iranian put out a Fatwa on Shilpa. Oh lord she thought this is the last bloody thing I need but the press praised her story and as usual the production team got no credit, sadly they never do.

What it did do was give her the entre into the inner circles of the rebel forces in the Islamic countries and more so to the top people in power. Her reference to

Afghanistan once again opened the door there and the Taliban announced that the story was a pack of lies and even offered to meet Shilpa.

The CIA in Langley jumped at the opportunity and the Shilpa crew grew excited, even Dalia who had never been in this situation now got into the spirit of the day.

"We are offering, via CNC, a safe return to the Taliban if they meet you in Peshawar. You will be shadowed by a small Special Forces troop but you will not be in touch with them or vice versa unless something extraordinary happens. We have a safe house in the town where a person will accompany you from the embassy that will be a Marine officer in civvies as one of your crew. Let's say Tony's assistant. You will follow his orders at all times in an emergency. Am I crystal clear?" said the deputy Director of the CIA to Darius over the phone.

Three days later Shilpa found herself on the road she had travelled eight years earlier in 1998. She talked a lot to Darius on the way about those days and he in turn told her about how they were tracking her. At 3 pm they entered the safe house where Tony and the marine set up the equipment.

"Listen mate," said Tony to the marine "I need to know your name even if it's a false one."

"Call me Myron, my family does and so do my friends," said the marine smiling.

Tony noticed he had a side arm under his shirt and what looked like a radio transmitter up his sleeve.

The Taliban were supposed to come at 4 pm but no one arrived. They waited and waited then at 6.10 pm the door opened and three bearded men walked in and said *"As-Salaam-Alaikum,"* the Arabic greeting meaning "Peace be unto you.

"Wa Alaikum Salaam," the crew replied.

Tea glasses were given out and pieces of fruitcakes that the Americans had brought with them. Outside in a tatty Toyota sat four members of the Special Forces viewing every move on a CCTV camera mounted in the roof of the safe house. What was extraordinary was the Taliban had requested a sweep of the safe house, which was permitted and in the process of setting up the equipment Myron had installed the remote camera for the truck to view the action.

Two of the bearded Taliban were the senior leaders the third was the translator who spoke perfect English, which Tony noted was a midlands accent so he was British. Oh Boy! Thought Tony and he whispered it to Darius who passed Shilpa a note.

"Well shall we begin?" Asked Darius

The interview was well prepared by the crew and they realised five minutes into it that the older man understood English as he was answering the questions before the man from the midlands had finished translation.

Shilpa realising this dropped the English and in Pashto asked the older man if he might try to speak in English, as it would save a lot of time.

"Where did you learn our language madam?" Asked the older man.

"In your country many years ago."

"I am impressed. Yes alright I will speak in English but my friend here will have to be told what I am saying," said the man who now introduced himself as Abbas, which means Lion or even frowning, or looking austere. He was austere.

"Why you people lie about us and the slave trade it is against the word of our prophet and all morality," said Abbas.

"That's not so. I want you to see the footage on the monitor and then tell me you are not involved in this trade and that you wish to raise the children to one-day fight against us. Tie bombs to them and have them walk into a café or police station," said Shilpa.

Tony then turned on the monitor and played the footage of Afghans trading women on the border with the Iranians. 12 year olds being beaten and raped.

The footage was from a video taken by an NGO worker on her phone who had disguised herself as an Afghan man.

It was noted that the British Taliban looked shocked while the other two didn't even blink. "This like you British say 'Humbug,' all rubbish lies!" said Abbas.

The other man then said something which the translator said "You are making this up we are very respectful of our women we worship them not abuse them. You people know nothing."

"Actually I do know a lot about you sir," said Shilpa "I was abused and tortured by your people for many years so do not tell me how you treat women."

Oh lord thought Darius this is trouble why the hell did she come out with this now?

Tony's experience also noted the tension and said time to change tapes.

The room was quiet and the three men went into a whispering conference and then got up.

"You will not leave this room or house till I get back. Who are you? You are not CNC," said Abbas.

"Yes we are look these are our credentials," said Darius. They all took out they CNC ID cards with ribbons and put them around their necks. Damn, Myron didn't have one. Abbas looked at Myron and said "Where is yours"?

"I must have lost it or it's in my bag we don't often use them as we have jackets that say PRESS or TV."

Abbas walked out and took out his cell phone, which he had concealed in his boot. Myron's check had been a bit slack. They all waited as he came back in and sat on the chair, whispered to the others and then they all sat quietly.

"Look what's going on?" Asked Darius. "We have a deadline to meet. Please let's get on with the interview. OK"

"No. Sit and be quiet," replied Abbas.

The people in the Toyota started to get anxious as they could feel something was going down but didn't want to react till all the ducks were in a row.

After ten minutes an old Chevy station wagon arrived with all the windows covered.

"You all come with us now to our safe house and we continue there," said Abbas.

"Sorry we are not moving from here," said Darius still acting the senior.

Myron had said nothing.

The doors opened and in burst two men with covered faces brandishing AK 47s about. "You come," one of them yelled.

Myron told them all to hold their places when suddenly there was a massive explosion that shook the house.

"Your people in the Toyota are dead mister. You think we are fools to not check you all out, what you think?" said Abbas.

Shilpa's throat went dry as desert sand, Dalia wet herself, Tony just stood in thought as to what to do next, Darius was stunned and Myron walked into the dark part of the room and said nothing.

"We are not moving," said Myron. He had his right sleeve to his mouth and spoke again "We are staying here and I advise you not to try and take us hostage. It will only spoil relations we are trying to build with you."

"You say lies about us and we will take you in. You bring much money to us as hostage. CNC is big company we will get a good price for you," said Abbas and the others nodded. Abbas walked out of the room to see the damaged Toyota, which was smouldering and body parts were all over the place.

Then the Brit spoke softly, "Listen mate do as he says, he is not kidding. He will kill you if your lot don't shell out soon. He has done it before and won't hesitate to do it again. They have nothing to lose."

"What the hell are you doing here? Long way from bloody Birmingham isn't it? Asked Tony.

"You wouldn't understand,"

"Try me," said Tony.

Noting the conversation the two men with the AK 47s dropped their guard. Myron seeing that, in a flash, pulled out his Magnum and fired 2 clean shots into the head of one and chest of the other. Then went out and ran into Abbas and shot him in the leg to take him captive. It was all over in about ten seconds.

Dalia wet herself again and Shilpa almost fainted, the tension had been too much for them all. They all collapse on the floor as a sound of a Blackhawk helicopter came closer. It was the sweetest sound they had ever heard.

Four Seals jumped out and ran into the house while three others scouting the place outside. Abbas lay on the floor bleeding profusely while Tony and Darius tore up some of his clothing and tied it to each side of the wound and one bandage over the hole to stop the bleeding.

When the Seals stormed in, one of them was a medic and had been warned by Myron about the wound so immediately dressed Abbas and gave him a shot of morphine that put him to sleep in two minutes. They placed him on the chopper and dragged the dead bodies out into the street and left them there as a warning. The other two Taliban were handcuffed and escorted to the back of the chopper where they couldn't move.

Dalia was shaking and in shock. The medic gave her a shot and a sedative to calm her down. Shilpa had been there before but still took deep breaths to stop herself from feeling dizzy. Darius was dry in the throat so gulped down a bottle of water; Tony too drank but a Coke. Myron was cool as a cucumber and took a sip of water, he was the last to mount the chopper.

The next day not only did CNC lead with the story but the entire American media including right wing channels accused CNC of using amateurs as reporters and being sensationalist, but they still led with the story even if it was to be negative.

CNC reported there was more to come and the CIA was delighted to have caught Abbas who was not just a senior leader but close to Osama bin Laden.

The entire crew was moved to the base hospital for an overnight check. None of them felt like eating the steaks placed in front of them. Abbas was in the hospital but in a secure wing. He was getting ready for the grilling that was to take place. The two other Taliban men were in a secure cell measuring 10x8ft.

"Oh Lord will I ever get out of this fucking country!" yelled Shilpa at about 3 am.

A male nurse came running in to see if she was having a nightmare. He sat next to her in her private room and they talked for over an hour and then he gave her a sedative to make her sleep. "Woo, lovely bit of stuff she is. Yea if only I liked women darling," said the male nurse to his colleague when he returned to the office.

15
THE REPORTER

"When you're wounded and left on Afghanistan's plains, and the women come out to cut up what remains, jest roll to your rifle and blow out your brains and go to your gawd like a soldier."

- Rudyard Kipling, reporting for The Times.

Within a week the team was out in the field again and this time they met up with the soldiers of the coalition. The answers from the men in the theatre of war were shocking.

When the interviews were sent to CNC in Atlanta and some to New York City people were aghast to hear and see what some of the soldiers were saying about being in Afghanistan It was titled:

"I WANTED BLOOD"

**Sound bites:

"I volunteered because I have always wanted to fight in a war because I hate radical Islamic extremists." *US Marine Corps*

"I hoped for everything a soldier dreams of — taking it to the enemy and fucking him sideways. *Soldier, British Army*

"The thing I wanted more than anything was blood! I wanted those people to pay! Look what they did to us on 9/11." *US Marine Corps*

"I volunteered so that when I could tell my grandkids -you live in luxury that I bought you fighting those pigs in Afghanistan." *US Army.*

The interviews brought sharp reaction from the Pentagon and the British MOD. The forces in Afghanistan announced a press lockdown.

Shilpa sorted out the people who hated the Afghans as much as she did but it was Darius and Dalia who made her see the plight was not just the Taliban or Al Qaeda it was the sad situation of the men, women and children in the region who didn't want war and had suffered for over 20 years. So Darius chose to do a story on the children of the country and the mothers. Dalia came across a story that was to shatter even the most hardhearted war hawks in the USA.

** From the Internet of real interviews.

CNC broke the story after the crew was ordered to a funeral of an eight-year-old girl. They thought it was a bomb or drone that had killed her but the story was one that even a Hollywood horror producer could not make.

Shilpa's report began with a cautionary note from the anchor:

Shilpa standing by the funeral party began her opening on camera:

"We were asked to this funeral because an eight-year-old girl was being buried. There is nothing news worthy about this in Afghanistan, but the 8-years-old girl whose story you'll hear and the pictures you will see did not make it to the 2nd night of her wedding. Yes let me say that again-her second night after her wedding."

'I don't know her name' and nor do I want to know in case I am questioned. A source called me to say this funeral was taking place and that I might want to film it. I thought this was a waste of time and told my producer so. He asked me to call back and this is why we are now here.

Voice-over with pictures of the area:

The story came from a village in Khashrood district of Nimruz province in Afghanistan. A medical doctor assigned in the main hospital in Zaranj city, the capital of the province who wished to remain unnamed confirmed the story:

VO-doctor:

"I was made aware of the incident and that it was too late to do anything for her. Also in remote area like this they didn't allow us to do anything."

Shilpa continued: (footage of the people and the mullah who was hiding behind a rock).

"The father was in debt to the mullah so he traded his daughter to the priest to have the debt forgiven. The mullah is in his late 50s and is the mosque man of the village where this incident happened."

** *From the Internet.*

(More video of the area and the mullah who refused to talk on camera)

"The mullah is already married and has many children.

The two families hold a tribal meeting, agree on the price that the groom's family pays to the bride's family, and they set a date for wedding.

I spoke to a war correspondent who remains anonymous, who broke the story, about the details as to what then took place, as he was able to talk to the family who sat there and observed this horror without doing a thing. Here is his exclusive report to CNC":

VO. Reporter:

"*The celebration party was over and the sun downed – the time to have sex (not make love) with the 8-years-old bride.*

The girl was just 8 years old and everybody understands the fact that she knows nothing about sex or wedding or making love or virginity or sexual related topics; not even at a basic level for two reasons, one being that she's just a child – not even a teenager and that in that part of the country, nobody knows anything about these things nor are they given trainings or education about a healthy sexual life.

The mullah takes off the bride's clothes as well as his own. Because of the Mullah's huge physique, which gave him a big penis, he threw himself on her and started to penetrate the girl's vagina.

After several tries that led him to failure to penetrate her vagina, the Mullah was frustrated.

He failed because the 8-year-old girl who was about to die was physically thin and had a very tight vagina opening.

Sourced from the Mullah's animal behavior, he took out the sharp knife that he always carried with himself in his pocket and tore apart the girl's vagina from the clitoris side upwards as well as tore it downwards towards her anus in order to make the vagina larger enough so he can enter his penis into her vagina.

Naturally, she started to bleed, but the mullah was too annoyed for not being able to have sex with her, to care for what he did or her bleeding or her wounds that he gave her. The girl had her scarf stuffed in her mouth, crying and trying to not raise her voice because others were there in the room adjacent to or outside.

It is a rule in some of the areas in Afghanistan that the groom brings out a piece of cloth that he cleaned his wife's hymen blood with it as a proof that the girl was virgin.

Mullah entered his penis into the girl's severely bleeding vagina and had sexual intercourse with her on a blood-covered bed, and then got up and cleaned himself with a cloth.

The girl, who now has lost everything, was bleeding and there was nobody to help her neither could the Mullah ask for help as it was a shame for him and the girl's family who were sitting over a cup of tea in the other room would kill him.

Our 8-years-old bride bled and went into a traumatic shock because of both forced sex as well as severe bleeding. She had lost so much blood, this I can tell for certain.

She bled and bled and early in the morning around 5 when the sun was about to rise, she passed away.

According to the Mullah, she was pale and her eyes were open when she died. The bed, as he described, was all red with her blood and she was lying in her blood only. No cloth beneath her was recognizable and everything was in dried blood because a whole night had passed on the blood. . Her eyes were open as she was shivering when she died and her hands were tied in a praying position, saying her death time prayer.

The Mullah called some people and asked them to clean up the mess around and prepare a reason to tell the others for her death. Because they were close friends or family of the mullah, they did whatever they could, including burning every piece of cloth that was bloody.

That morning her family mourned her death in the saddest manner without looking for proper explanation about her death, and then took her to wash the body as a religious ritual.

Because the Mullah had a great influence on the village, none of the women who washed the girl's body dared to ask or seek the reason for the wounds around her vagina.

By 10 am or so they rallied the now-dead 8-year-old bride to the graveyard and buried her.

Her life ended.

Shilpa on camera:

"Another doctor that I asked in Zaranj said that he wasn't aware of the case, but he remembers that he used to treat the now dead bride when she was 4 or 5 years old.

This doctor also asked me to not name him anywhere but only said that he was deeply saddened that incidents like that still happen in Afghanistan."

He called it one of the reasons why Afghanistan is not going forward: People's idiocy, uncivilized behaviors and traditions.

This story reached me as it was told the exactly the way it happened by the Mullah to a very close friend of his after the girl's dead body was buried. According to the Mullah, he had a "bad conscience" about it.

Well I suppose it's putting it mildly that the Mullah had a bad conscience about it. This country is a mess to say the least and it's not just the Taliban or Al Qaeda that are to blame it's the thinking mainly of men and uneducated women who are at fault. I must thank our anonymous reporter for this amazing vivid report. This is Shilpa Moray, CNC, somewhere in Afghanistan."

Atlanta went crazy when they saw the story and put it out worldwide. CNC and British TV censored parts of it but the Russians put it out with all its gruesome details and so did some of the European networks. It shot Shilpa Moray into star status and she loved it. The real reporter was lost in the shuffle and so was the crew especially Darius whose idea it was.

Darius called Atlanta and asked to be brought back. The whole crew needed R&R and so a few days later a flight was arranged to Karachi and then PIA to New York and then Delta to Atlanta. Shilpa and the crew were now world famous and so they all agreed to ask for a massive raise in pay.

16
BEYOND THE R&R

While Shilpa and the crew were enjoying their 15 minutes of fame, the prisoners from Pakistan were being flown to a secret prison in Saudi Arabia. The CIA and the army were interrogating Abbas, the Brit and the other man in the safe house.

It turned out the Brit was Adrian Cook from Birmingham now using the name Mohamed Ali. The other was a Pakistani Mustafa Haq a former IT engineer who hated the Americans and joined the Taliban. He hated women and was a closet homosexual, only known to a few, as his services were vital to the Taliban.

Adrian was an idiot at school, always bottom of the class and never had any friends to speak of so one day he went to the local mosque 'just for a laugh' and by the end of the Friday prayer he was asked by some young men to join them for dinner. It had been years since Adrian was asked to dinner so he went along to one of the semi-detached, three bedroom house of a boy called Iqbal Patel from Pakistan where his family had laid out a mutton biryani dish with vegetables and parathas. Adrian couldn't remember when he last ate a meal so tasty and rich.

"You like our food?" Asked Mrs. Patel.

"Champion it is misses. Ta very much" said Adrian in his Birmingham accent.

From that day on he hung out with his new pals every day after school even though his classmates teased him for being a 'Paki lover.' One day when the classmates decided to beat him up. He went to his Muslim friends bleeding at the nose and bruised around the buttocks and chest.

"Who did this to you Aid?" asked Iqbal

'Leave it. Bunch of wankers," said Adrian.

"Is it because you is out with us then?"

"Suppose so…"

"Right who was it. Come on you is our mate and we stand up for our mates don't we?" said Iqbal.

The other five all agreed. They went home brought out their cricket bats and went looking for the gang that beat up Adrian. When they found them there was no warning, Iqbal and gang just smashed into them with the bats and broke one bloke's nose, cracked a rib on another and beat the living daylights out of the rest, beating their backsides and legs.

From that day on no one messed with our Adrian and he in turn went to mosque every Friday till his conversion six months later. He now started to watch the Internet with speeches in English from the Taliban and Al Qaeda. It was a long time before he saved up enough money to fly to Pakistan and join the Taliban taking the name of his favourite boxer Mohammed Ali. His usefulness was that he was a translator as he had learnt Urdu in England and was working on Pashto. He was liked and needed.

As for Mustafa Haq he came from an educated upper middleclass family who had made money in oil and business but a local cleric had asked for his help with the computer and soon he was under his spell and was told he could be God's soldier by working for the Taliban with his skills. What he wasn't told at the time was he would have to also learn to kill and his first task was to kill a young girl who insisted on going to school. It took him days to get around to it but he also realized if he didn't then he or a member of his family would be dead.

So one morning he walked to her house and as she came out pointed the gun, looked the other way and fired. Then turned around to see her fall and ran away before anyone could come out to see what had happened. He was inducted.

The three men sat in cells 10x8 on their own. They were led to individual cells and the interrogations began. Abbas was questioned gently at first then as he was uncooperative the slaps began, then the kick in the shins and soon the shouting and the beatings till his face was bloody and raw. Still he offered nothing to speak of.

As for the other two, Haq and Ali, they gave the forces all the information that was needed. Where the cells were, who was there, what were the plans for fighting the Pakistan army, destroying the Allied convoys and so on. Haq even gave them the passwords to their computer systems.

Why? The interrogators had the names and addresses of their families in the UK and Pakistan and they would make life hell for them to the point of taking some of them out in a way no one would suspect. This scared the living daylights out of the two men who in turn were offered decent food and allowed out for an hour each day whereas Abbas was in a cell without any light and just a small window which streaked in a shaft of sunlight for few hours a day.

Within days of getting the information from Haq and the Brit Ali drone strikes were ordered and a platoon of soldiers sent into a village to destroy the cells. The villagers came out to greet the soldiers and offered them opium as a gift from their stores as they had nothing else to give for their thanks. Many of the younger soldiers took it and the officers turned a blind eye to them.

Back in America Darius and Dalia were on leave in San Diego and Shilpa had decided to go there as well but stay in a hotel near the sea at the La Jolla Inn on Prospect Street where she could walk down the swank street and shop at the same time. She also felt lonely and thought of Tito so many miles away and of her father and if the dreadful Shalini was making a move on him now she wasn't there. Thanks to the cheap phone calls she spoke to her dad almost every day but she couldn't say a lot except she was now a reporter on CNC and her dad was so proud of his daughter that he told all his friends and with the repetition of the stories on the CNC International channel everyone now knew Shilpa Moray of CNC.

The phone rang in Darius' study. "Hello, oh, hi Shilpa how are you?"

"Lonely. Would you and Dalia like to have dinner with me tonight?"

"Well you know Dalia is not too well but if it's OK with her I could come or better still you come over," said Darius.

"No not if Dalia isn't well. You come to me and let's eat in the BBQ place near my hotel. It's got a fire pit you know the one," said Shilpa.

Darius went to ask Dalia if it was OK for him to go out. "Well I suppose so after all these years I have to trust you with her don't I?" said Dalia. She had never forgotten how she found them almost naked in the hotel years ago.

Shilpa was waiting at the table near the fire pit with a Grey Goose vodka and tonic she rose to greet Darius who gave her a peck on the cheek and ordered a Bloody Mary without Tabasco.

"We have come a long way baby. Who would have believed this scene a few months ago," said Darius raising his glass to her.

They talked and talked about the past even though at times Darius felt very uncomfortable but realized she needed to do it. All this time working together she never brought up their past or the stories behind trying to buy the TV station and their affair. She had to get it off her chest and he sat there like her shrink and listened for over two hours. In between they ate a meal of roast duck and trifle with sherry.

Around 10 pm Shilpa insisted on paying the bill and they took a walk down Prospect Street to where the seals gather on the beach below. It was quiet and the seals were asleep. They strolled down the quay to the far side where they were alone and Shilpa took his hand. He held it firmly and stared out to sea.

"I miss you a lot these days. Not when we're working then there was so much to learn and study. By the way if I haven't said it before you are a brilliant producer. In fact you should be in front of the camera and not me. Thank you for everything," she said and tried to kiss him but he moved his head away.

"Can't go through all that again Shilpa. Dalia is my rock and I really do love her. We had a quiet life until you came here and I am not complaining. It's got my adrenaline going after years and the money is very welcome. I also see a side to Dalia I never guessed she had, she is a brilliant researcher."

"Yes she is I have to admit," sighed Shilpa. She took Darius' hand and kissed it for a few seconds and smiled at him.

They walked back to the hotel where Darius kissed her on the cheek and walked home, which was only a few blocks away. Shilpa lay on her bed and wondered if working with Darius was a good idea. Right now she needed him.

She spent time on her own going to the zoo, Sea World with Dalia and Darius, to the concerts at Symphony Hall and plays at the Old Globe. Suddenly the lust for Darius was gone and she began to really like and admire Dalia. People started to talk about a ménage a trios but nothing was further from the truth.

After two weeks the call they expected came from CNC in Atlanta and they were ordered back in 48 hours as a story had come up and the CIA were involved.

17
INTO THE UNKNOWN

The VP of programmes, Damon Dallas, came into the conference room with a paper, which he said, was of great importance, written by the head of counter terrorism of the CIA.

"This piece by Robert Grenier is stunning not because of its content but because we, on the board, agree with just about all of it – Grenier was head of CIA's Counterterrorism Centre in 2004–2006, he had to have been intimately involved with many US efforts in the Middle East he has been in direct conversations with the top leader in Egypt and other Middle East counties. I am going to paraphrase his account for you now you can read it on your own later," said the VP Dallas.

"Events in the Middle East have slipped away from us. Having long since opted in favour of political stability over the risks and uncertainties of democracy, having told ourselves that the people of the region are not ready to shoulder the burdens of freedom, having stressed that the necessary underpinnings of self-government go well beyond mere elections, suddenly the US has nothing it can credibly say as people take to the streets to try to seize control of their collective destiny.

All the US can do is "watch and respond," trying to make the best of what it transparently regards as a bad situation."

"Some of you there may recall Porter Grass and Jose Rodriguez sacked Robert Grenier in early 2006, for being soft on torture. Not only does this column condemn many of the interventions in Pakistan, Iraq, and the Middle East generally in which Grenier was personally involved. But it suggests one reason behind his removal at the CTC may be a very American devotion to democracy," said the VP.

"So here is the story I need you lot to go to the Middle East and find out what is happening as we think one of these days there will be a revolution and we may not be part of it. I also want you to look into the banned Muslim Brotherhood in Egypt. They were banned 30 years ago but they still have cells and will rise again according to your friend at the CIA."

"What's the story Damon? What are we really looking for? It's a mess there and has been for over 60 years. Talking to the Brotherhood gives us nothing and to what end?" Asked Darius.

From the back of the room a man who wasn't at the table rose and said, "Folks, I am Richard Manton a Deputy Director at the CIA and this is my operation. Indirectly you will be reporting to me via your own office but in this case we are calling the shots. Now if anyone doesn't want to be part of this please leave the room now and no questions will be asked. This will not be an easy operation so please feel free to walk out. Once you stay you are here for keeps," said Manton and then sat down and no one moved. He waited a full minute and the stood up again and explained the plan

The crew of Shilpa, Darius, Dalia and Tony were set up as friends going on a cruise down the Nile to see the ruins of Aswan. This is the site most people go to see at Lake Nasser, as it was the genius of the Russian engineers that took the ancient statues and pillars of the temple at Abu Simbel and replaced them so that the dam water didn't cover them up. This is a land of white sand and ritzy hotels and the biggest moneymaker for Egypt. One experiences a blend of Nubian and Egyptian culture, but for Colonial Victorian grandeur, the Nile from the deck of the Old Cataract Hotel would be hard to top. On any given day you will see arguably the most awe-inspiring temples from ancient Egypt.

They entered the opulent Old Cataract Hotel with its view of the river and the white sails dotted on the grey water. At $300 a room with breakfast the crew was thrilled they were not paying for it. Not only did it have an outdoor pool but also one of the most luxurious indoor swimming pools in the world with mosaic covered pillars and water just cooler than bath water. Attendants to give you fluffy white towels and if need be rub you down with a massage.

The strange part of the trip was that they were told that a person would meet them and then they would know their mission. "Well we might as well make the most of this while it lasts," said Shilpa never one to give up on a bit of luxury. She went down to the indoor pool with Tony and slipped into a bikini. Tony could only stare and wish he wasn't working with her. Her 5–7" body was looking better than it had done when she was 30 and now over 40 she looked remarkable after the surgery in London. Tony realized the bulge in his trunks was giving him away so he dived into the pool and went on to do four straight laps. Shilpa in turn swam on her back where her breasts seem to float on the water in a provocative way and did she know it. Others in the pool also noticed and whispered to each other especially the women.

A middle-aged woman came out with a towel as soon as she saw Shilpa get out of the pool and covered her with it. "Madam please follow me so I can help dry and relax you," said the woman. Shilpa followed thinking this was going to be a massage. They entered a massage room and the woman quickly closed the door and said, "I am Yasmin your contact. It's strange but we had a feeling you of all people would come to the pool here. We need you to meet the man who you are to interview. He is coming tonight to a café down the road and I will be the one to lead you there. Please dry yourself and tell the others. I will call you in your room at 7 pm so please ask the others to be ready." She opened the door and walked out leaving Shilpa to think is this for real?

At 5.30 pm the crew met in the bar and Shilpa told them what had happened. Tony said he was going to carry a miniature camera with him to record the meeting; it would be in his jacket lapel.

Just before 7 pm the phone rang in Shilpa's room and they were alerted to come down to the lobby where the middle-aged woman met them. No names were exchanged but they were led to a car, an old Morris Oxford from the 1950s. They drove for several miles to a small café on the side of the road. It was dimly lit with some naked bulbs and a strong smell of tobacco and tea permeated the room. A man in a light linen suit stood up and greeted them in the traditional way. The crew responded and they sat down to some tea and snacks that were served within minutes. Everything had been carefully orchestrated. A man then entered the room and looked around.

"I am Kamal Musa and I will be the one to take you to the Brotherhood and Al Qaeda leaders but you must not do anything that I am not informed about otherwise I am not responsible for your lives," said Kamal.

"There is a movement to get rid of Mubarak and his corrupt regime. Their friends in the Arab world, Hamas and Al Qaeda are helping the Muslim Brotherhood to start a revolution and topple the regime. He has been in power too long and with the help of the Americans. He is almost 80 and he has raped this country of billions and we want to have a real democracy in Egypt and not this phony one the Americans say we have. Tomorrow I will take you to interview the people you need to see and then you can report on what is really happening in this country," said Kamal. He rose from the table and wished them a good night "Please eat here the food is better than your posh hotel."

The following morning, at 5.30 am, Kamal and Yasmin came to the hotel to pick up the crew. Tony had already transmitted the previous evening meeting to the office in Atlanta and from there it went to Langley. Richard Manton was impressed at the fast delivery, but now came the big event.

The six of them drove for what seemed hours over the desert road. The sun had come up and by 8.30 am it was getting hot but the old Morris didn't have air conditioning. It reminded Shilpa of the Ambassador cars in India made from the 1956 Morris Oxford for over 50 years. Finally some tents appeared in the distance and they were told that they had arrived at the destination.

The wind had picked up and the dust and sand was beginning to fly into their eyes. The group was led by Kamal followed by Darius, then Tony, Yasmin and finally the two women. The man in a white kaftan spoke directly to Darius and was surprised to learn it would be Shilpa who would actually do the interview. He went into a conference with the other man who was dressed in black fighting fatigues and they decided the questions had to be asked by a man. So now the CNC group went into a huddle and they decided they would go with it but later do cut a -ways of Shilpa asking the questions and reacting. Bloody absurd thought Darius but then they had to get on with it.

Shilpa sat next to Darius and Tony set up two cameras —one for the interviewer Shilpa and the other on the heads of the Brotherhood and the Hamas leader in a two shot. So now he could get Shilpa's real reactions and get both men. Tony was behind the camera for the two men so he could pan and zoom as he liked and the other one was locked off.

"Thank you for allowing us into your home and granting this interview," said Darius.

"God be with you and your crew," said the headman. It was on purpose no names had been exchanged. That was part of the deal.

"When did you first think of forming this alliance with Hamas?" Asked Darius not wanting to waste time.

"My brothers in Gaza and I have talked for years about this and now we have come to realize that it is together we fight for the freedom of Egypt and Palestine. We are united in this matter and divided we fall," said the headman.

Darius asked if women would have to cover their faces when the MB took over.

"We will not make a law but it will be up to them to cover themselves or else some men may take it into their hand to force the matter and we will be powerless especially if the man is the husband. But we will tell the women they have to answer to God in the next life."

They spoke of banking and foreign investment, they avoided the question on alcohol, as it would affect tourism and avoided questions about higher education for women and finally came to Israel.

"The Muslim Brotherhood is a vociferous critic of the Zionist state. Although we long ago renounced violence as a means to bring change in Egypt, we say those facing occupation must resist by all means. The Palestinian militant group Hamas sees the Brotherhood as a spiritual leader."

Then the Hamas leader spoke "We see the Israeli people as racist, colonizing, expansionist and aggressive entity and we say the Palestinian issue is the most serious Egyptian national security issue today." He ignored the 1979 treaty and all else that had been done by the two countries.

"Now sir we have something to ask of you. We need you to talk to your network and give us one hour to put our message over to the world and especially the American people," said the Hamas man.

'What are you joking?" Asked Shilpa.

"Woman you keep quiet. I not speak to you," said Hamas man.

"I am sorry we can't allow you to speak to her like that. I know we are in your country and your customs but there is a limit. I am not trying to offend you but she is as shocked as the rest of us. We can't ask for such a demand nor will it be given. Sorry we can't do it," said Darius.

"Really so you think we are joking? Asked the MB man

"I am sure you are not but it's an absurd request. No network worth its salt will do this for any organization, unless you buy time on the network and that could cost over a million dollars," answered Darius.

"OK then we let you go but the two women stay with us. May be your network think they are worth one million dollars eh," said the Hamas man.

"Sir you can't do that it's not worth the price. I will stay behind and you let them go," said Tony.

"You are technician, worthless. How you say two a penny. Now women worth a lot more than one million," said Hamas.

Something was said in Arabic and three heavies came and grabbed Shilpa and Dalia and dragged them out both screaming and kicking, while Hamas man held a gun to Darius' head. Tony a fit 60 year old grabbed the MB man by the throat and said he would kill him if Hamas man didn't put the gun down and release the women. The Hamas man turned and shot Tony in the leg and he collapsed on the floor bleeding profusely.

"Oh Jesus, get him some help. Do you have a doctor?" yelled Darius.

"You were ready to kill us a minute ago and now you want us to get a doctor?"

"Yes please get someone!"

"We will show you mercy," Hamas called out in Arabic and within a few minutes a man attended to Tony who was almost fainting with pain. The dressing took ten minutes as it was a clean wound, as they say, in and out of the leg but bloody painful.

All this time Kamal and Yasmin had not said a word. Darius turned to them but they both just shrugged their shoulders. MB man came up to them and said in Arabic take these men back and see they do what we have asked otherwise your families will hear from us. Yasmin whispered the message to Darius who in turn was lost as to what to do. This is not a training a TV producer gets. He asked to see where the women were being held and it was granted. They were both in a large tent with three other women who had their faces covered. Darius even wondered if they were men.

"I will be back soon and I want a report on the women every day and I need to speak to them twice a day if you want me to do your bidding," said Darius very firmly to the two men. Tony was put on the back seat of the car and the other three sat on the front bench seat and drove back very slowly. As soon as they were out of range Kamal made a call to Cairo to say that he had attached a GPS tracker to the Hamas car and they were given the readings. "Brilliant Kamal, well done son," said Tony and Darius shook his hand.

They didn't sleep that night and were up with Atlanta and Langley till the early hours when Darius said, "Guys get some rest there is nothing you can do right now."

The hotel doctor attended to Tony and gave him a painkiller so he could sleep.

Darius noticed that Yasmin sneaked into Kamal's room. Oh well it goes on all over except I hope they really are on our side.

18
THE BARTERED BRIDE

All hell broke loose at CNC and the CIA they had no idea these 'loons,' as they called them, would do something like this. "Do we have an ID on the Hamas car?" yelled the Deputy Director. "Yes we do sir, but there is movement. Our car in going in to the Gaza Strip while the other one is moving to Israel, that's odd isn't it sir? Asked a junior. "God only knows. Watch them very carefully." Which car were the women in? That was the $64,000 question!

CNC decided to sit on the news, but the feeling was there was a traitor or spy for another network in the office. The News Director Tom Sloan got a call from his counterpart at CBS. "Is this story true about the kidnapping of your girls in Egypt"? Asked the CBS man. "Christ your place leaks like a sieve Tom. What's the scoop and do you want us to sit on it if so for how long?"

Tom didn't spin the story but told them the whole story and the truth that CIA were involved and it had gone all the way to the President. "Yes, sit on it please and the girls as you put it are in serious danger for their lives." So CBS agreed and they all sat on the story waiting to hear from Egypt.

At 5 am the following morning, now over 24 hours had gone by since the crew had left Shilpa and Dalia at the camp, the phone in Darius' room rang. It was the hotel phone.

"Yes, hello," said Darius

"So my friend how you are today? Your wife and other woman are OK but I warn you if you don't come with answer in 48 hours there will be serious consequences." He hung up the phone. Smart bastard thought Darius now I can't trace the call coming through the switchboard; the system was an old 1960s board.

Within minutes Darius woke up Tom Sloan in Atlanta and gave him the message. The news was sent to the CIA and to the head of CNC in New York. America had woken up early that morning and now it was time to wake up the President. "We are going to bring those ladies back gentlemen and I don't care what it takes. Even if its firing a million dollar missile at a ten dollar tent. No one messes with our women is that clear."

In the morning Shilpa and Dalia were wrapped in blankets but still shivering in the early desert air. The sun had just risen over the horizon and the few fowls and animals started to greet the dawn. The cock crowed, the dogs barked and the camels coughed. Shilpa put her arm out and touched Dalia who in turn held her hand and moved closer so their bodies could warm each other.

"OK, OK, wake up we have tea then we move," said a young Arab who knew some English. The women slowly woke up and were offered cans of water to wash their faces and they both rubbed their teeth with the forefinger of the right hand. Hot tea was given to them and a piece of bread that Shilpa said was a naan in India. After fifteen minutes they were in the jeep owned by the Hamas on their way to God knows where.

Four hours later the two women were brought into a hut, which was part of a compound of Nissan huts left by the Israelis years ago. They were marched into a room with a camera and a black backdrop and told to kneel there.

"Now good ladies you will talk to the camera and we will let the people in America know you are with us and treated well. If you try to do tricks we will beat you till your flesh shows from your skins. You do what I say and you will be OK," said the Hamas leader.

Before that ordeal a tray of rice and kebabs was brought in with dates and cans of warm Coca Cola, which surprised the women. They ate the food and then asked if they could use the loo, which turned out to be a hole in the ground not any different from what people use in India or Afghanistan. Shilpa was OK with it but Dalia wished she had constipation but sadly it was the other. When they returned they were made to sleep which they did for over four hours, then told to have a bath with a bucket and mug but no soap. After that they were given clean kaftans and allowed to brush their hair. The Hamas wanted them to look good on camera.

11 pm Eastern time in Atlanta a PA came running into Tom's cabin to say he needed to see this coming over the satellite. When Tom got to the gathering room he saw Shilpa and Dalia in kneeling positions talking:

"We wanted to let you know that we are alright and are being treated with respect and kindness. Its really important that you allow the Brotherhood and Hamas one hour of air time to make their case against the state of Israel and the regime in Egypt. We have been promised they will let us go immediately after the broadcast airs but it must air two times in a 24-hour period without commercials. Please do this or our lives are in danger. Thank you," said Shilpa.

Then Dalia spoke to the camera, which remained, on a two shot. "Darius I love you. Please talk to the powers that be that we will be killed in 48 hours if the request is not met and that we are in a situation where the Hamas army is not joking." She then held up a newspaper, which showed the date as November

23rd 2006. It was the Wall Street Journal of that very day. The CIA couldn't place where the message was coming from as the GPS was on the other car and that was in a parking lot in Jerusalem now and had been there for 24 hours with no one near it. They had lost the women.

Darius paced his room and so did Kamal. Yasmin was on the phone to the Egyptian foreign ministry in Cairo. "They are useless," she said and then added they blame us for being so trusting of these bloody people. Even so the minister of Defense was sending out word to their troops in the desert to keep a look out for the Jeep with 2 foreign women.

The phone rang in Darius' room and this time the voice was speaking in broken English not the Hamas man of the tent.

"You come to answer us in 24 hours or your wife dies. This no joke, understand now?" said the strange voice and then hung up.

Darius got on the phone immediately to New York and told them what happened. They in turn called the CIA and the State department. Within two hours Darius had an answer to say CNC needs to meet the party in person at a neutral location with Darius and Tony there and then negotiate a deal.

Darius had no way to get in touch with the parties so he just had to wait for 22 hours when the call came again and this time he said there could be a deal but he had to speak to someone who had the power to say "yes." An hour later a call came, it was the man from Hamas but this time also on the line was a man from Al Qaeda.

They agreed to meet at a very public arena in Alexandria, Cecil's Hotel. Now stripped of its 1920s grandeur and made into a "modern hotel" but safe in terms of security and any underhand play by the kidnappers. 48 hours later the president and VP of CNC flew down with an executive, who was really a senior CIA operative. Darius and Tony were there 24 hours earlier to greet the party and discussed in detail all that had to be done.

1 pm came and went and there was no sign of the kidnappers. The CNC team drank more coffee and talked. 2 pm came and went and they started to wonder if this was a hoax. Every few minutes they turned to the entrance but none one came towards them. Finally at 2.35 pm a group of 3 men, two dressed in Kaftans and one in a safari suit came to the CNC table and simply sat down in front of them.

"There is no need for names and introductions," said the Hamas man who Darius and Tony recognized immediately and whispered to the CNC and CIA man as to who he was.

The man in the Safari suit spoke "We are not here to bargain. Let me be clear we want your airtime and you can have your women. No long discussions am I clear?" he said in perfect English and in an English accent. This was not a Middle East Arab. He was either part English from his complexion or an English convert.

"What exactly are you going to say in this hour that you want? I am not having any hate speeches or anything that will cause your people or followers to incite a riot in the UK or US or for that matter India or Pakistan where we have a strong presence. If you want to talk about your dissatisfaction with us and make a 'legal case' then we can consider it. But any inflammatory stuff and I will cut you off at once," said the CNC President.

There was silence amongst the kidnappers, then some whispers and a lot of nodding and shaking of heads.

"You cannot vet our script or program we go on 'live' for one hour and then we hand over the girls," said the man in the safari outfit.

"No, the girls are to be in an Escrow holding position with a neutral party to be decided. Once the broadcast is over they are released to us.

"No, no, they stay with us and we release them to you after one hour."

"Sorry that's just not on," said the CIA man. "We insist and there is no compromise on that. Am I crystal clear?"

"And if you don't do what we ask we will put the execution of the girls on YouTube for the world to see. Am I crystal bloody clear?"

"Sorry we can't accept that…"

Before the CNC president could finish the group got up and walked out of the lobby.

The CNC team was left looking at itself. They sat in silence for a few minutes and then the CIA man took out his phone and made a call. "They are all bloody mad," said Darius shaking his head in disbelief.

That night no one really slept at the hotel. At 6 am Darius got a call to say he and the others should tune into their website and see what was being offered. Darius quickly woke up the others, booted up his MacBook Pro and tuned into the website mentioned by the voice on the phone. There they saw Shilpa and Dalia on their knees facing the camera and were told to speak.

"Please don't let them do this to us. They are going to cut off our heads if you don't give them what they asked for. Please spare us we are not spies for the Americans but they don't believe us," pleaded Shilpa. Dalia was shaking with fear and tears were rolling down their eyes. Just then a head covered with a black scarf came on and said "I will call you in one minute and I must have your answer. We will do what we will do, no conditions."

Screen went black and Darius said "You have to give it to them these bastards are not joking," he shouted at the corporate men.

The phone rang and the CNC president picked up the phone and agreed to the deal but wanted see have the women in his care before the broadcast and the telecast could be done from Cairo the next day. The man in the Safari suit refused and said that CNC was not in a position to dictate and told them to switch on the channel again.

When the picture came up they saw Shilpa and Dalia still kneeling but facing away from the camera. Then within seconds two scimitars came down on the women's neck. One had to be done again on Dalia's as it wasn't a clean cut and the blood gushed out of the top of their torsos.

Darius threw up and the others just sank onto the beds in shock. Darius' vomit made the others also feel ill and the CIA man went into the bathroom and spilled his guts into the toilet. Tony, tough Tony, was actually shaking; the CNC team was in shock. No one had ever witnessed anything like this before. After about five minutes the CIA pulled out his special phone and made a call to Langley to report what they had seen and being on YouTube they could watch it over and over again if they wished. Darius started to get the shakes and the hotel doctor was called. Not too much was said except he had a very bad shock and was given a sedative and told to go to sleep. As they saw Darius fall asleep, within minutes, they all asked for a sleeping pill and went to their rooms to sleep it off except the CIA man who wasn't in the best of shape but had to wait for Langley to get back to him.

At 8 am the phone from the US came and the CIA man in Alexandria took the call. He was told that at the time the delegation had come to the hotel a tail had been put on the kidnappers so they knew where they were except no one thought they would execute the women so quickly. A Special Forces operation was being organized and it would be put into action within 6 hours from an aircraft carrier in the gulf.

Eight hours later when everyone woke up they were told the news. "Lot of bloody good that's going to do for my wife and Shilpa, "said Darius "I want to personally hang the sons of bitches when we get them here."

The doctor came by again to check everyone. Darius' blood pressure was very high so he gave him another sedative to make him relax and go to sleep. The others were on the phone to Atlanta, New York and Washington. Within hours the Egyptian government sent their defense minister to the hotel and a truck full of soldiers to guard the place. The minister asked them all to move to a army rest house, which would not be known to anyone, for their safe keeping. Two Jeeps carried the team over to the old King Farouk palace, which was used as a hotel and army base now. It has magnificent grounds and its the place the young despotic king lived in from 1936 till 1953 when he was kicked out of his own country in an army coupe led by Colonels Nasser and Nagib.

Food was brought to their rooms but no one could eat except Tony who tucked into a plate of steak and chips. More calls and the Egyptian major who sat with the CIA man made a call and then told the team something was happening.

Blackhawk choppers had been seen flying into the desert so he assumed they were the US forces on their way. Silence again. CIA was monitoring the action from Washington and Langley and the 'situation room' at the White House was full with the President, VP, Secretary of State and others watching the action on the screen –a live TV show. It was frustrating for the team in Alexandria that they had to keep waiting for phone reports. They all sat in silence for the next 90 minutes when the phone rang.

"Mission accomplished!" was the sound on the CIA speakerphone. "We have 4 dead and 6 prisoners. 2 injured on our side but not serious. Here is the good news, the women are alive!" Massive cheer went up in the room. Darius fell to his knees and prayed. Tony, with tears in his eyes said, "I am not normally religious but would someone like to say a prayer of thanks please?"

The CNC president and others went on their knees and so did the major and they recited the Lord's Prayer and then gave thanks for the safe return of Shilpa and Dalia. But what the hell did they witness, that execution was real wasn't it?

16 hours later the women and the CNC team were reunited in Alexandria at the palace. Shilpa and Dalia were visibly shaken and clearly needed care. They had been attended to by the medics on the choppers but insisted on getting back as soon as possible to their team and loved ones. So the choppers landed near Alexandria harbor and an Egyptian army jeep brought them to the Farouk palace where Dalia flew into Darius' arms and Shilpa was first greeted by Tony and then hugged by the rest of the team.

After a through exam the two women were given strong sedatives and told to go to sleep as they had already eaten with the US forces after the rescue. They slept for the next ten hours without waking up.

19
DANGEROUS LIAISONS

The investigation went on at Langley with the two women, for four days, with them giving their statements: On the day of their execution they were asked to plead for their lives and then the screen went blank. When the contact was made again the viewer's only saw the backs of the women but they were not Shilpa and Dalia but two Arab women who had committed adultery and were to be stoned to death but then they were used as the substitutes. The sheer cold bloodedness of the act shocked even the hardened CIA staff. "Christ man what have we come to in the 21st century?" asked a staff member.

"We were in the room when it happened and were told to watch but Shilpa and I both closed our eyes and the sound of the blade hitting the necks is something I will never forget for the rest of my life," said Dalia.

CNC and the CIA made an undisclosed deal with Shilpa and Dalia of $1,000,000 each and $250,000 to both Darius and Tony but only $20,000 to the two local operatives. Now flush with money and newfound independence Shilpa wanted to move on. Darius and Dalia chose to go back to San Diego and try to settle down again to a peaceful life and pay off the mortgage on the house.

Shilpa felt the need for a 'hot weekend' and she was in a position to hire the hottest guy on the net so she booked herself into '2 Bunch Palms' in California, one of the most expensive resorts in the country, and hired Jose to be her date for four nights. Tall, dark and handsome he was but he was also known according to the website to have amazing stamina in bed. What more does a girl want thought Shilpa!

By the end of the third day Shilpa was exhausted and completely relaxed. Jose made her forget the ordeal of the past months and she in turn made Jose feel he had fallen in love but she was soon to forget him after a phone call to her father who asked her to return to India.

Her life was a series of complications now. No base, no real job, still connected to the CIA and MI6 and her escape from India in 1998 still hanging over her head. She wanted to see her mother but not land in jail doing it.

Shilpa decided to write to Jill at MI6 in London to see if she or the firm could do something for her to return to India without any hindrance. Jill was not very forthcoming on the matter but asked Shilpa to give her a week and then call her again. She had read and heard about Shilpa's movements with CNC and was impressed at what the woman had achieved in a short time. It seemed like the kidnapping in Afghanistan was paying off in a strange way now.

Jill had always been fond of Shilpa so she arranged a meeting with the Director and a senior official from the Commonwealth office to discuss Shilpa's return to India. After about thirty minutes they came to the conclusion that Shilpa had physically changed so much after her ordeal with the face lift that a new passport under another name and a British citizen could enter India without any problems. Four days later Jill called Shilpa with the good news and asked her to come to London to collect her new British passport.

A week later Jill smiled as she handed over the new passport and when Shilpa saw it she broke into a big smile. She was Shalini Ashok Kapoor. Born in Calcutta in 1970. Both her parents were deceased and she had been living in the UK since 1998. The irony of the name *Ashok Kapoor* made Shilpa smile. It was the name of the star and former lover who had committed suicide after running arms to the Taliban.

"We had considered you being born in Leeds or even London," said Jill "but then we realized a sharp person would pick up on your accent which certainly isn't English as you would definitely not be speaking the way you do, charming as it is."

Shalini threw her arms around Jill and hugged her for over a minute with tears in her eyes. "I want to do something special for you Jill," she paused and thought and then said "Why don't I take you to India with me and give you the vacation of a lifetime. Please let me do that for you," she pleaded.

"I couldn't take that it would be considered a bribe in this place. I thank you for the thought but no," said Jill.

Shilpa booked herself into the St. James Court Hotel owned by the Taj-Tata group in India. This lovely guesthouse of Queen Victoria was used as a place for dignitaries from foreign lands like Ambassadors and Prime Ministers. Then in WW1 as a hospital and finally as a hotel which was run down and had old majors and captains housing there after retirement. Eventually in the 1980s the Taj group bought it, renovated it to its old glory and made it into a five star hotel.

Shilpa walked in St. James's Park alone and relaxed planning her trip to India. She hailed a passing taxi to take her to Harrods, as she still wanted to buy something worthwhile for Jill and the Director.

The following day she was at the HQ and walked into Jill's office unannounced as she still had her ID card to pass security.

"If you don't take this I will tear your eyes out. I mean it Jill," said Shilpa

Jill didn't say a word just took the package in the dark green Harrods's bag and pulled out a waist length mink jacket by Valentino. "Oh my God! Oh, lord!" is all Jill could say. "I am going to disclose this I can't take something like this it's so, so bloody fabulous!" cried Jill.

"No you won't. I am a private and personal friend and this is your birthday present which I happen to know is next week and as I am going away it's an early pressy. OK?"

Jill kissed Shilpa on the lips and then on both cheeks. Shilpa was flushed and turned her head away for a second and then kissed Jill on the lips but this time for several seconds. The two women looked at each other and then stoked each other's faces.

"You are a lovely person Shilpa. Want to have dinner with me tonight?"

"Sure love to but first take me to the boss I have a gift for him as well."

The Director took the Harrods's bag from Shilpa and said, "Oh you shouldn't have but let's see what it is?" There was no shyness on his part. He pulled out the dark brown Gucci brief case; took it in both hands and said "Well my wife will have to be told not to save up for my Christmas present this year. This is so handsome and will replace my 30-year-old civil service bag today. Thank you so much but really it wasn't necessary." He walked up to Shilpa and to her surprise kissed her on the cheek.

Jill had moved from the King's road and now lived in Drayton Court in Drayton Gardens, South Kensington. Her family had had the flat since the 1950s and when the place went condo she bought it for a song. Now she had flat with four bedrooms, large kitchen, living room, dining room, toilet and one bathroom. Victorian didn't believe in a bath every day and the tradition went on for decades till the 1970s when the younger generation started to put in showers and add a second bath to their houses.

The two women sat in the kitchen nursing Blanc de Blancs from Bolney Estate one of the leading lights in the English wine firmament. Shilpa watched Jill put together a salad, with a cut of filet mignon beef, which she pan-fried and served medium rare. Shilpa had never really been attracted to women but now she felt a strange pang as she observed Jill's 'English rose' looks, which reminded her of the films she saw from the 1950s. Her face was like the soft colour of peach, which had hardly any makeup. She was slender but with a firm round bust and legs that reached far past the normal eyesight.

Shilpa walked over to the kitchen counter and put her arms around Jill from the back. Jill didn't react at once, paused and then wiped her hands on the apron and held on to Shilpa's hands. She then slowly turned around and took Shilpa's face in her hands and kissed her gently, then more passionately. Both the women were breathing heavily and wrapped in each other's arms.

"My God! What are we doing?" Asked Shilpa.

"All I know is I have wanted to make love to you since I first met you," said Jill.

Holding on to each other they almost danced to the bedroom where they started to remove each other's clothes and then couldn't make up their minds as to who was the dominant one so a wrestling match took place on the bed. They suddenly broke off and started laughing. Shilpa began to play with Jill's nipples and in turn Jill stroked Shilpa's crotch. They both leaned towards each other and began to kiss; the lovemaking was sweet and gentle.

When they woke up in the morning they realised that the curtains were open and the light was still on. Someone peeking probably had a great show, which made them both smile. "I want to spend the day with you so I am calling in sick," said Jill.

"OK, let's brush our teeth and go back to bed," said Shilpa. So they both did.

20
RETURN HOME

"I don't know if we will ever meet again but I will never forget you or these past four days, "said Jill as she kissed Shilpa at Terminal 5 for her British Airways flight to Bombay or Mumbai as some locals insisted on calling it now in 2007.

'I love you like I have never loved another person before. I want to be with you now and in fact I almost cancelled this morning when I woke up," said Shilpa her eyes like the English weather, damp and cloudy. She stroked Jill's right cheek. They hugged and stayed that way till the announcement for the flight came which jolted them into reality. Shilpa walked away towards the security barrier then turned around and ran back to Jill kissing her all over her face while the other passengers stared at the highly emotional scene.

"Come with me please," pleaded Shilpa. "I am scared of what will happen in India."

Jill didn't say a word but simply walked Shilpa to the barrier and kissed her on the cheek. She watch as her lover went pass the barrier and got lost in the crowd, then walked back to the parking and drove to work.

The landing in Bombay was a pleasant surprise. The new airport was so much better but still as so often in Indian public buildings the floor tiles were cracked and not replaced, potted plants needed water and several pots were broken. Painting on the walls left a lot to be desired but still a massive improvement thought Shilpa. Her first class bags came early and she breezed through customs and immigration with her new passport. She kept reminding herself she was now Shalini and not Shilpa.

As she exited into the courtyard she heard her father call out to her. He broke through the barrier and ran towards his prodigal daughter. Wearing sunglasses *Shalini* could pass off for an Indian film star. People started to crowd around Ajit and Shilpa but the driver parted the way as he moved them to Ajit's new BMW.

For the next two days Shilpa sat with her mother and told her some of her experiences in Afghanistan and in France but very little about her CNC experience even though it had reached the world. Her mother pretended she didn't want to know but was happy her Shilpa was safe. She was told about the passport and not to whisper a word to anyone absolutely anyone. So at home she was known as *Shalini* madam to the servants and to friends and relatives as long lost cousin/ niece *Shalini*. It seems no one recalled Shilpa after all she was dead or lost to the world and this lovely lady from UK was just "too good yar."

Everyday Shilpa phoned Jill, sometimes twice a day. Knowing the nature of Jill's job she was cautious but times the urge to hear her friend's voice was so overpowering that she even called her on her special line. "Please try not to call this number as it's monitored and only in an emergency call me here, "said Jill after the third call in four days.

"I really miss you so much," said Shilpa. "I sleep in a bed of chastity and you are miles and oceans away. In the morning when the day breaks I feel it's my heart. I recall a sonnet by the bard, which said something like; *'All days are nights till I see thee and nights bright days when dreams do show thee to me.'* Come back to me my gorgeous Jillian," wept Shilpa. She had crushes and flings when she thought she was in love but never like this. Now she had the need for someone at her side, a companion and a lover; this time it was a woman.

Mumbai as it was politically called was not the same as the Bombay she left in 1998. Mumbai was an environmental mess. The roads were too small for large trucks and cars; the garbage was all over the place and the corruption rampant at every level in the political and business classes. The parties that controlled it kept talking about it being "the Singapore of India" but as a TV anchor pointed out they can't even fill in the thousands of potholes on the roads. In Singapore potholes are filled in within 48–72 hours or the official in charge is questioned.

Shilpa/Shalini had no friends to visit or she would have to give herself away. After spending three days with her mother and seeing she was healthy Shilpa was bored.

Ajit noticed the restlessness in his daughter so suggested that she gets involved in the building boom that was going on in India especially in the city of Mumbai. He had invested a big chunk of his millions with builders who had put up tower blocks and were minting money, as there is such a shortage of space especially in south of the city.

He introduced her to a partner, Sunil Bhosle, as his niece from the UK and asked him to teach her about the business especially selling properties and gaining access of old properties for a song and then developing them.

One such property was on the posh side of town, a 4,000 square feet house, near the Governor's mansion. A Parsee family owned bungalow. In fact it was divided up between several cousins who inherited it from their mutual grandparents. Many of them lived abroad now and just an old aunt and her spinster daughter now lived there. The Parsee community is littered with spinsters and bachelors living with ageing parents or siblings. They have the lowest birth rate in India and in fact the Parsee panchayat-it's so called governing body- is offering to pay for the education of a second child in the family so as to increase its dying population. In 1941 the community was over 100,000 strong, in 2008 it was about 60,000 and going down daily. Many Parsees went to the UK, US, Canada and Australia. There are some Zoroastrians in Iran today but they are less than 10,000.

The family Dorabjee were once wealthy importers and had a stevedore company in the city but as the restrictions came into force over the years especially in the 1970's the company lost money and eventually the younger generation moved on to other businesses so all that was left was the house. The large house was built in 1898 when the family was working closely with the British to import and export products like silk, opium, exotic herbs and ivory from the Far East and Africa. They in turn also exported bales of cotton to the mills in the north of England. Over the years the family became millionaires.

In 1990 the Heritage Committee (HC) of Bombay put what seemed like a curse on the building by making it a heritage property. This meant nothing of the outside could be changed and if it had to be sold then permission was to be granted by the committee. The family objected and several letters were written to the committee and to the housing minister with no results. In fact after the first letter there were no replies to the objection. The fact was that a lot of renovations and extensions had been done to the house since 1950 so it really didn't qualify to be a 'heritage' property.

Ajit's builder partner Sunil Bhosle was a self-made man. He started life as an agent and part-time contractor's supervisor. Learning the trade from the bottom up he finally got the confidence to try building on his own. He went to his original boss who was now retired and was told he needed 3 lots of people on his side- contractors, politicians and the mafia to do the dirty work.

So Bhosle tried to educate Shilpa. "Dear girl, to make it in this business you have to start by going to functions and parties. Don't worry if you are not invited. In India yar everyone is invited so just go like you know people. Then once in you will always find people you know so say 'hello' and they will introduce you to their friends. Soon these friends will invite you especially if they know you can do business with them. Then you invite them to a small dinner and then when you want to spend more money a bigger dinner and get one or two politicians to come. They will if they know it's good for them; if you know what I mean," said Bhosle.

The two sat across a table at the coffee lounge of the Oberoi hotel, overlooking the Arabian Sea, in Bombay mixing with trendy rich and foreign businessmen. Bhosle continued his talk.

"You know my first building was outside Mumbai. I bought land from a poor farmer. I paid 25,000 rupees for an acre then I got three acres more, which made the poor man happy and me even happier. Then I met local MLA, you know member of legislative assembly and I told him he is my partner to get all planning permission passed. Then what problem I am having. One NGO took objection to my cutting trees and making housing for middle class people so I am stuck. Vat to do. This again where politician is useful. He gets his 'gunda' friends to help. I told you, no, you must have mafia on your side. Then these people are giving good beating to NGO, useless people always making trouble for us. Then they stop and my work is going on," said Bhosle in his self-taught English; pouring his tea into the saucer and slurping it loudly.

"So how much profit did you make if you had to pay off all these people and partners?" asked Shilpa.

"Lady I tell you. Good profit. First you add 30 per cent to your costs before your profit because you have to make up for all the 'hafta,' you know bribes, you have to pay off and then add 30 per cent for profit. Why you think cost of building is so high in India? Labour is nothing it is all this bribing and nonsense that is making life difficult," said Bhosle shaking his head.

"How high is the corruption?"

"Oh too much high lady! All the way to the top of chief minister's office and more if it's a national project. Why do you think the door to the CM's office is always open to builders even people like me?"

"Is my father then involved with all these people?"

"No, he is keeping clean I am the front man for our business. You dear lady will be front for me with clients as I am not too polished and speaking good like you."

Shilpa thought I hope to God dad is not getting me to go from the frying pan into the fire. She thanked her new mentor and went home to contemplate what could be a new life in Mumbai not her old Bombay.

Sunil Bhosle had told Ajit More that the Dorabjee property with its acre of land was a gold mine for building a major structure in Mumbai and the profits would be colossal. What he hadn't taken into account was the building was heritage and then when they approached the authorities to take it off the heritage list they found that not only was the house under the rule but so was the entire property.

To top that the Heritage committee had been disbanded and a new one was yet to be formed, so they approached the Dorabjee family with a plan.

They would give them Rs. 500,000 now with a MOU for the rest as and when the property would be released. Bhosle would do all the 'arrangements,' code for bribing (now known as *Speed money*) and then when that was done he would give them the equivalent of US dollars two million in cash and check. The cash would be 'black' money and deposited to any bank abroad of their choice. India has two economies, 'white' and 'black.' White being legally obtained income and black being non-declared cash obtained in trade, service, or sale of property. It's alleged that the largest numbers of Swiss bank accounts belong to Indians.

Bhosle went to his MLA friends now high up in the state government and asked for the site to be removed from the heritage list. He was told by his friend now a minister of urban development, "Listen boss with all this computer business our powers are being cut. Not like in the old days and a push of the pen could change everything but let me see what can be done," said the minister.

He told Shilpa/Shalini they were now on the final lap. "No problems yar!"

21
THE DORABJEE FAMILY

The Dorabjee cousins heard about the property being sold and suddenly two of them flew in from the UK and USA. No one had taken an interest in the old place but the sound of millions of dollars made the two of them "homesick" for the family property. The one from the USA, Aspi, was an accountant who had blown his saving on the US stock market crash of 2001 and the other from the UK was a travel agent, she had worked for a major agency for 20 years. Armity was in her forties and divorced whereas Aspi had two kids in college and now in his late fifties was looking at retirement if he could afford it one day.

The full time residents of the house were; Freny Dorabjee in her nineties and her spinster daughter and Aspi's younger cousin Roshan who was in her fifties. Freny's other two children were in the USA and Australia. Now letters and phone calls started to pour in from Freny's kids and her late brother's children of whom Aspi and Armity were two of three; the third one, Sammy, living in the north of England and cut had himself off from the family for years.

Three of the five bedrooms hadn't been used for years and so when the 'foreigners' arrived and major clean up took place but the walls still had peeling paint and damp. Freny had to hire a new maid for the time and a cook for the new residents. As soon as Aspi arrived he made an appointment with a lawyer to see what could be done about the offer made by Bhosle.

"Are you mad accepting an advance from the builder? Who told you to do that and then sign a MOU?" said the exasperated lawyer. "Never do something like that."

"We haven't yet accepted the offer," said Aspi.

"Good. The bastards will take you for a ride. They give you the advance then when the time comes all sorts of excuses will come about this and that then the price will go down and eventually you will get about fifty per cent of the value. I will put you in touch with some agents and work the sale around to some more people you should get about twenty crores for your place," said the lawyer.

"What that in real money?"

"In dollars about four million easily. One crore is about 200,000 rupees today."

Aspi was stunned he had planned on getting a little more than two million. This would take care of his retirement but he was forgetting about the capital gain taxes and the expenses.

The Dorabjees were sitting down to a late lunch four days after the cousins had arrived when the maid came in to say there was a lady, a 'madam lady' at the door.

Aspi got up to see who it was to find Shalini there smiling as if she had known him for years. "Hello you must be Aspi from the US. I am Shalini representing Mr Bhosle who made you an offer some weeks ago."

Aspi was charmed by the looks and the warm greeting Shalini gave him.

"Oh yes please come in we were just finishing lunch. May we offer you some food?" said Aspi.

"I am fine thanks please finish your lunch and I will wait for you."

About ten minutes later all four family members came out and sat with Shalini as tea was brought out in a tray and set before her.

"Let me get to the point miss," said Aspi. "We are interested in selling but not for the price or deal your man offered us. I have just come from the US as you know and we already have an offer of four million dollars or in your money twenty crores. So there is no comparison."

'Well you have some major hurdles before you can get the twenty crores I can assure you. First and biggest is your heritage status. My people can smooth all that out but it will not come cheap and you can check that out with whoever you like. Mr Aspi let me tell you to move a sheet of paper in the clerk's office you need to pay otherwise nothing will happen. Try it yourself and then if you can't call me and we will see what can be done," said Shalini with a smile that melted Aspi on the spot. Where the hell did she come from? They weren't like that forty years ago thought Aspi.

Shilpa reported to Bhosle who smiled and told her to wait for a week they will be back and this time we will get them.

Aspi called a few old friends and talked to them about the deal. Almost all said the woman was right that corruption is rampant and nothing will get done without money and we are not talking a few thousand rupees these days as one pal told him. Aspi told the family and also those who were still abroad that this was not a simple buy sell deal.

Within two days another four builders came to him and the price offered was twenty five crores by a major builder who claimed he had the municipality in his pocket and if Aspi and family were to sign off he would give an advance of one crore (a crore is Rs.10, 000000-about $200,000) and balance when his work of clearing everything was done.

Shilpa/Shalini waited in the wings for the next two weeks. In the mean time she sold two flats to an international company and took a commission of rupees five lakhs or ten thousand dollars. Not bad for a month's work she thought.

Late on a Wednesday night the phone rang at her flat, it was Bhosle asking her to go to the Marine Plaza hotel to meet Aspi Dorabjee. She thought this was odd but he wouldn't ask for a meeting like this unless it was serious.

"Well Mr Aspi what brought this on at 9.30 pm? Asked Shalini.

"May I call you Shalini mam? Asked Aspi. Shalini nodded.

"We have talked this over with family and I want to say we will go with you but my sister Armity who you met doesn't like you. Jealous I think nothing more. So I wanted to meet you in private and see what we can work out. Is that OK?"

"Yea sure. What do you have in mind?"

"We want to sell the whole property but my cousin-sister, Roshan, thinks as she lives in India now she can own the whole place as most of us live abroad and when my aunt dies she being my cousin will take it over. She talks about 'being to the manor born' and all stupid romantic ideas. She has no idea of what it takes to maintain the property and even if she did rent parts of the place out how long will she be able to handle it. She is already in her late fifties," said Aspi.

"Where do we come in?" Asked Shalini.

"I want you to get the clearance from the heritage committee or whoever is in charge when the HC are not operating and then make us an offer we can't refuse."

"What if your sister objects and won't sign off?"

"Our grandfather's will say majority action will be taken and it's a trust will."

"Let me talk to my people and I will get back to you but I am warning you now from what I know of Indian bureaucracies it won't be cheap. We are in an election year and all these damn babus want to make a killing as they have no idea where they will be placed next."

"How much are we talking about?"

"Not sure but lakhs or in your US money thousands of dollars."

"Jesus Christ! All I want is a win-win situation where we all get our due share and live our own lives. Roshan can get herself a lovely flat somewhere or even move to Poona and live comfortably for the rest of her life," said Aspi sipping his Diet Coke and looking sad.

That night Shilpa sat on her bed and wondered about Jill. It had been a week since either of them had called each other. It was 11.30 in India and 6 pm in UK so she picked up the cell phone and made a call.

"Hi, hello this is a surprise. I thought you were so engrossed in making money you forgotten me," said Jill.

"I think about you twice a day," giggled Shilpa.

"I miss you a lot and feel neglected when you don't call," said Jill.

"You have no idea how much I miss you and London, Jill my darling. I want your body wrapped around mine and your breasts on my lips and your hips pressing into mine, I want you so much darling," sighed Shilpa.

"Kiss me. Kiss my breasts, touch my face, and put your fingers inside me. Are you doing that to me now?"

"Yes I am. I am licking your thighs, now biting your nipples and I am so deep inside you and you feel like wet silk. Come my baby come."

The breathing got heavier and heavier from each end and then Jill screamed "AHH! Oh my God, oh my God. Oh I haven't come like that in ages. Wow, this is almost better than real sex. No wonder people pay these phone sex people so much. Wow!"

Shilpa was still panting. She hadn't had an orgasm but still felt satisfied that she had helped Jill climax.

"I really love you Shilpa. Do you think I can come and visit you? Will we get some private time together?" Asked Jill

"Actually I will go nuts if I don't see you soon. Let me send you a ticket, don't worry about the cost and just email me when you can take some leave," said Shilpa.

22
LOVERS IN MUMBAI

BA's flight from London to Mumbai landed at 11.30 am a few minutes before schedule. When Jill walked out of the airport under the canvas canopy she was greeted with a scream from Shilpa who ran out of the barrier and hugged her friend and lover like a fourteen-year-old schoolgirl. The two of them actually jumped in the air much to the surprise and shock of the multitude of taxi drivers and relatives waiting for the passengers to come out.

Without thinking Jill kissed Shilpa on the lips which made even Shilpa blush but she didn't say a word and put her arms around Jill and walked her to her father's BMW. As they drove out Jill said the same thing millions of tourists and first time visitors say of Mumbai -that the stench was appalling and what is it? Smells like a toilet. Shilpa smiled and told her she wouldn't notice it after a day.

When they reached Shilpa's flat they both turned to one another and hugged for over a minute.

"I need to have a shower and get the smell of the plane off me," said Jill.

She was led into her own room and the water heater was turned on so she could take a leisurely shower and be fresh for her lover.

When she walked out of the bath Shilpa was stretched out on Jill's bed with a kimono open in the front. That extraordinary body for all to admire and only Jill's for the taking, which Jill took advantage of at once.

They made love for the next hour and finally Jill fell asleep in Shilpa's arms. It was 7 am before Jill woke up again and Shilpa was now fast asleep next to her with a smile on her face.

The maid had made Jill coffee and an Indian omelette, *a poro*, which consists of spices, fried onions, tomato and coriander. She sat overlooking the sea at the waterfront known as Worli Sea-Face. The Arabian Sea is grey in these parts thanks to the pollution but the sea breeze was pleasant at 8 am. The landline rang and made Jill jump. It kept ringing and the maid said that was a private line for Shalini madam, which she wasn't allowed to answer. Jill picked up the phone after the 10th ring.

"Who this is? Asked the male voice.

"Hello, this is Jill. I am Shil...I mean Shalini's friend.

"Oh, Jill. This is Ajit More your Shalini's father. I am glad you corrected yourself it's very dangerous in India to use the other name," said Ajit. "Welcome to India my dear. I have heard you were very kind to my daughter some years ago in London. I was calling her on her private line as I have business with her today, is she near you?"

"No I am sorry she is asleep."

"Wake the lazy cow up and tell her it's me I must speak to her now. Please my dear."

A sleepy Shilpa picked up the phone and spoke for a minute with her dad and then without a word walked into her bathroom and turned on the cold shower. When she had done her ablutions she realized her bed had not been slept in so she pulled back the covers and punched the pillows so the maid wouldn't suspect anything. She would have to do this daily from now on to either her bed or Jill's.

"I want you to come with me to this meeting," said Shilpa to Jill over breakfast.

They drove to her father's new offices in south Bombay an area known as Nariman Point; Built in the 1960s and 70s, a densely built area of 10–12 story buildings, unimaginative and now unkempt, mostly used as offices and some residential with one of the highest square footage rates in the world.

"Hello, hello you are the famous Jill. Welcome my dear to our humble abode. I am so happy to see you. I can already see Shilpa's face glowing," said Ajit More.

"Well thank you and its lovely to be here. I have wanted to come ever since my uncle who was here in the 40s talked about it. He left in 1949 with Mountbatten you know," said Jill her smile lighting up Shilpa's face.

"You are going to witness what the British left for us in India and we in turn have made this stew into a holy mess; that is our unnecessary bureaucracy. I am sending Shilpa to the ministry of Urban Development and there to meet the under-secretary of the ministry and see if we can get our work done with this envelope," Ajit put his hands on an envelope on the desk and handed it to Shilpa.

The ministry for the state of Maharashtra is in Mumbai called the Mantralaya at the southern tip on the city. There the legislative assembly sits and so do all the offices for the different ministries. The condition of the offices has to be seen to be believed; paint peeling off walls, damp patches from the monsoon rains, dirty furniture and they are over staffed, underworked and underpaid so little to no work gets done in time. The minister's offices have air conditioning and decent furniture, which include plastic covered sofas and large glass coffee tables.

The sight that really gets noticed is the paper work in bundles all over the floor, on top of cupboards and on the desks of the clerks and junior officers.

"Hello, you are Bhosle's daughter?" Asked the minister in Marathi as Shalini walked in with Jill behind her. Shalini shook her head and answered in English "No sir, I am Ajit More's niece. Mr Bhosle is a partner to my uncle," said Shalini.

"Who this lady?" Asked the minister pointing to Jill.

"This is my friend from the UK Jill Adams. She is working with me on this project," said Shalini pointing to Jill who did a '*Namaste*' to the minister. It was clear at once the man was not comfortable with a foreigner in his presence.

They all sat down and tea was ordered. Idle conversation took place till tea was served and then Shalini said, "My uncle has sent you a package for the help you are going to give us. I hope we can rely on your good faith to do the needful,"

"See lady it is not so easy to do this work," said the minister quickly taking the package and placing it under his bottom. "You are vanting to take this site off heritage list but to do this we have to show cause no? So vat cause you is showing?" He said in his thick Marathi accent, which Jill was finding difficult to follow. He then went on to explain it is not only him that has the power but the Director of Town Planning and his assistant and deputy and then the records clerk etc.

"Are you saying we have to take care of all these people?" Asked Shalini

"Oh yes why not and then we have to take care of people above us as well. This is not an easy matter in India. You are coming from foreign now or you are Indian? Asked the minister.

Shalini gave him a nonsense story about being born in Bombay and educated abroad it was so full on nonsense that Jill had to look down and cover her face with her hankie making out she had a cold. But Shalini was cool as a cucumber and just started to flirt with the official who loved it.

When she finished her piece of fiction Shalini crossed her legs slowly in front of the minister at which point his eyes dropped very quickly to the middle of her body. Then in Marathi he asked "You will take some dinner with me and we can finish this matter in a nice way. Vat you say?"

Oh God! Thought Shalini here we go again. I wonder if dad knew this would happen, the bastard!

She smiled and said yes but I have to bring my friend, as she is alone in India.

"Array, no problem yar. I will also bring a friend. We have a good time," said he in Marathi.

Jill was amused when she heard about the invitation. "Let him put a hand on me and I will break his hard dick in two," she said with a grin. "We'll have some fun with these yoyos."

A white Ambassador car came to the flat at 7.30 pm to pick up the ladies and take them to an apartment on the sea front at Cuff Parade, one of Mumbai's best areas, now spoilt by a stinking fishing village that the politicians allowed to develop on the beach and reclaimed areas. The two ladies were dressed in traditional saris with revealing 'cholis' or tops, which were backless.

The minister rose as the women entered the room followed by a manservant.

"Hello my dear ladies. How you are doing? This my wery good friend and cousin brother Vijay Kulkani, he big man in sugar cane and likes to live sweet life if you are getting my meaning," said the minister trying to be funny and impress the ladies.

"Lovely to meet you both," said Jill. Shalini didn't say a word just smiled.

Kulkani immediately patted the space next to him on the sofa and asked Jill to join him. Kulkani was a tubby man about 5'-6" with dyed black hair but the white roots showing up in sections of the scalp. He had a heavy moustache and gold and diamond rings on both hands. Not exactly a man Jill would fancy. Just the thought of having sex with him made her feel sick. Well it wasn't going to happen.

They all made light easy conversation and Vijay kept offering the ladies drinks of a really good Nuit St. Georges 1992. He really had no idea of the vintage just that it was red French wine. The women loosened up and they all laughed at the men's silly and sexual remarks till dinner was served. The four sat down to a meal ordered from a restaurant consisting of mutton biryani and tandoori chicken, which Jill really enjoyed. Meal over she asked to go to the bathroom to wash her hands. Vijay got up to show her the way and then stood outside the door till she came out at which point he pushed her against the wall and pressed his body on her and kissed her lips.

"Please stop this," said Jill calmly and pushed him away.

"Lady Jill I give you too much plezure tonight and give you nice prezent if you nice to me," said Vijay and again pushed his pelvis into her. Jill took a deep breath and suggested they go to a room.

In the dining room the minister had moved over to the sofa and asked Shalini to sit with him. He took the front of the sari in his hands and dropped it in her lap revealing just her *choli* and the cleavage of her breasts.

"You are too much good looking Shalini. I desire you all day. Please come with me to bedroom. I am not animal I will make you happy," he said with a face of a puppy begging for a biscuit.

"I am sorry I have my period but you can touch my breasts if you like," said Shalini hoping it would satisfy him.

He ripped her choli, breaking the hooks and stared at the gorgeous 34C cups in front of him. His lips went down on her and at the same time unzipped his pants and started to play with himself.

Shalini pushed him away and looked at him straight in the eye, "I'll do this for you but you better do my work in the morning," she said in a no nonsense tone.

"Oh yes no problem," he said and dived for the lush breasts and climaxed within a minute. Then flopped back on the sofa and closed his eyes.

In the bedroom Jill had laid Vijay out on the bed and given him a hand job looking away most of the time having told him she was having a period. He in turn closed his eyes for the three minutes Jill played with him but kept muttering he wanted oral sex but Jill ignored him. He started to snore as soon as he climaxed. Jill walked into the bathroom and scrubbed her hands. As she walked out she bumped into Shalini who just shook her head revealing her naked breasts. Shalini too washed and when the two met outside the bathroom they decided to catch a cab and go home.

"I hope to God this rubbish was worth it to you Shilpa. He bloody well better do your work in the morning," said Jill feeling very irritated and nauseous.

Two days went by when Shilpa took Jill around the sites of Bombay: the Gateway of India, Hanging Gardens, which are a poor relation to the original. They ate at the Sea Lounge of the Taj Mahal hotel and walked the dirty beach at Juhu where they ate fresh coconut and bhel, an Indian spicy savoury dish. She also made sure Jill was taken to the top leather shop, Adamis, where she bought really good designer replica bags. At Punjab House they bought westernised silk kurta-pyjamas and pashmina shawls. Jill said, "It's been Christmas in summer."

On the third day Bhosle called to ask if the work from the minister had been done. "Yes for sure and he got a bonus from us," said Shalini. Within ten minutes another call came from Bhosle to say his man reported nothing had been done. "What did you say to him? He is doing nothing of our work," said an angry Bhosle.

"I need to go and see him myself," said Shalini.

She literally pulled Jill by the sleeve and called for her driver to take them to the Mantralaya. Shilpa was known for her no nonsense style so she stormed into the minister's office with the clerk protesting behind her and broke into a meeting.

"I thought we had a deal sir and you have not kept your word," said Shalini who had switch names again.

"It is taking time. Please you are interrupting meeting now. I am too much busy. Take her out," yelled the minister to the clerk. Jill strode in and made everyone sit up and take notice.

"Not so fast sir. I am part of the deal and if something isn't done soon," she paused and went up the minister and whispered in his ear "I will have you for rape within the next 24 hours. I am not joking."

The minister turned to his colleagues and said in Marathi "Explain to these ladies here nothing is done in two, three days. In time it will be done."

One of the men got out of his seat and said, "Madam, I am not knowing what it is you need but sir is correct to say all works in India take time. One-two days are nothing. Fast work is one to two months. He will do your work."

The two women took a deep breath and looked the minister in the eye and walked out. As soon as they left the door there was loud laughter from the office. Shalini hesitated to hear the minister say "What fun we had with these girls yar. Too good yar! What they think I am?"

Shalini was ready to walk back into the office but Jill held her arm and indicated they should leave.

"Shilpa darling we have been had by those bastards. That Vijay even offered me a present," said Jill

"Oh I forgot a parcel came for you yesterday and I put it on the side. It may be your gift."

When they got back to the flat they called Bhosle and gave him the report and then looked for the parcel. It contained a velvet-lined box with four large diamonds in it. Jill was so excited she wanted to get a ring and one for Shilpa so they drove off to Ajit More's jeweller; everyone in Indian has a jeweller, to get a couple of rings made.

Mr Javeri, the jeweller, examined the stones very carefully under a magnifying glass and then said "Very good quality. You get them in Amrika?"

"No I think they are Indian diamonds given by a friend," said Shilpa.

"Diamonds? No, no madam this very good quality Zirconia from US I think," said Javeri.

"What? I can't believe this!" yelled Jill in a voice the whole shop heard.

She closed the box and walked out of the shop with Shilpa trailing behind.

"Four days in India and I have been screwed every which way," said Jill.

"Except you know the real way," smiled Shilpa.

Shilpa was embarrassed and knew she had to make it up big for Jill. In the car home she held Jill's hand tight for the entire journey. When they got to the flat she walked into the bedroom and made love to her friend for the next hour. The phone rang at 3 pm to ask if they could join Ajit More for dinner as he had heard of the incident at the office and wanted to talk to the girls.

To their surprise Bhosle was at the dinner and they were told that now the matter would go to the Director of Town Planning (DTP) and then to his deputy and then to his assistant and all this would take some time.

"What is some time here?" Asked Jill.

"Who knows? Only they know," came the answer from Bhosle.

"How do you do business here with so much corruption?"

"We do and we know this is how money is made by these *Netas and Babus* in India. That is life. Do you know it's not just them because these people often have to buy their positions for crores, in your money Jill that is over 100,000 Pounds and then they have to get it back. So how? Corruption and they have to pay the party coffers as well," explained Bhosle checking his English for Jill's benefit.

"One friend of mine was offered a parliamentary seat in a rural area but was told he had to get over 20 crores (\$ 5 million) for the party in one year. In rural area how you are going to do that with farmers who are committing suicide because they cannot pay their debts? So when there is a big land deal in the process these bastards go for the higher numbers and squeeze whatever they can. So in this case we are dealing with a hot property, heritage, so these buggers will take all of us for a ride as they have calculated what it is worth and they will extract ten percent from us. Those days of 500 and 5,000 rupee bribes are over madam. Any way we will make our profit but in the mean time we have to pay out and that is why so many small builders are out of work now or their building not finished," sighed Bhosle.

Jill and Shalini (now in Bhosle's presence) sat in stunned silence. They were hearing about the tip of the iceberg. The entire mass underneath was yet to be discovered.

23
THE WRANGLING

To say Roshan was an unhappy, bitter woman would be an understatement. She spoke to her former boyfriend on the phone to see if he could give her some ideas as to how to beat the cousins. Now a middle aged spinster she was petulant and peevish with the world for having lost her early love, a customs officer who was 'straight' and didn't take bribes hence lived on his government salary. Her parents had hoped that she would marry a so-called 'Parsee blue blood' after all the Dorabjees were considered aristocracy in their heydays. After that she had an affair with a man she worked for and he in turn had promised to marry her and divorce his wife but that never happened, besides she was older than him.

Roshan was jealous of the cousins and envied their good fortune in living abroad and having the courage to take a plunge in a new country. She had never risked anything in her life. She hadn't even bought a flat or small house as an investment. Now the anger and envy rose to a peak knowing she could lose the house and security of her home.

Roshan had her own plans, as she was not a simpleton as her cousins thought she was. She in turn went to see a lower order clerk that she knew thinking he would guide her to the right people to stop the sale of the property. He in turn took the box of sweetmeats she had brought him and said he would pass her request on to the next man who would help her.

She wrote a letter to the Collector as she had been told to do but no reply was forthcoming. She then went with a cousin who was a retired police officer to the Mantralaya, seat of local government, to see if she could get an interview with a minister or state secretary. The cousin used his title to get into the offices where they were treated with respect by being offered cups of tea and told to write in to 'so and so' with copies of death certificates and wills. It took Roshan days to get them together from old files and then make copies. All this was done and sent by registered post. Then she waited and waited for the next three months.

Sometime later when cousins Aspi and Armity were having lunch with Roshan and her mother they were told that she was talking to some 'big people.'

"I went with our deputy commissioner Kambatta to meet the minister and they asked me to give them a letter and some papers which I did so I think our work will be done now," said Roshan.

"How long ago was this?" Asked Armity.

"Oh, about 3–4 weeks now but you know how slow everything works here," replied Roshan.

"Four weeks are you bloody joking Roshan. This means they have taken your papers and shoved them in the waste. What are you saying? I don't suppose you gave them anything?" Asked Aspi.

"Of course not I am not one for bribing, they showed me and the DP lot of respect and even gave us a cup of tea." said an irritated Roshan.

"Then forget it. You seriously think getting a former police officer that has no clout now and you sipping tea with a babu are going to get your work done? You are so naïve. I am really pissed off," said Aspi.

Roshan pushed her chair back from the table and walked out of the room, thinking I will get them just you see. Aspi then turned to his sister Armity and said "Look I have some people working on this and yes it will cost us money but in the end it will be a win-win for all sides. You just have to trust me on this."

Roshan not satisfied with the argument she got from Aspi went to see her deputy commissioner and ask him to help her again.

"Listen Roshan," said Kambatta shaking his head, "if you think these people are going to do something for nothing you have another thing coming. Wake up yar, these people buy their chairs and have to make up the money within a few years otherwise they have no idea where they will be in years to come. It's the system so join it or step aside."

Roshan fuming left Kambatta and went to see a former 'collector' she once knew. He in turn suggested she sees his former clerk, Ravi, who now had a mid-level position. She walked into a typical government office to discuss the names of the property card and the 'heritage status' of the house. The room was painted a light green but about 10 years ago so it was fading in patches. The roof leaked so large patches of mould had appeared on all four sides of the small office and in some parts the dust had attached itself so fungus was growing. No one seemed to care. A slow fan was circulating the warm air and the floor hadn't been swept in days.

"Namaskar Raviji," said Roshan in Marathi and then continued in the same language. "Collector sahib told me to come and see you about my problem. I have brought you some sweets for your family."

"Thank you madam. How I can help you," replied Ravi in English.

Roshan explained her problem to him for ten minutes and then he asked her several questions and in many cases kept repeating the question. She then went on to ask him to remove the names of the cousins from the property card only to find they were not on it but their parents' names were on it. She smiled to herself and said in Marathi "If only my name and my mother's name is there and not my relatives who are alive then I assume the house is mine. Correct?" Asked Roshan.

"Not sure of that but if your relatives don't live in India and do not have any claims to the property then you can justly claim it but they could file a case against you," said Ravi chewing a *paan, betel leaf,* and spitting in the waste bin. "My suggestion is you don't say nothing about property card till you are sure to sell the property then you can bring it up."

Roshan thanked Ravi and left the office feeling very confident that she had made a score against the cousins.

While Shilpa was drinking coffee with Jill at Café Coffee Day by the sea a call came from Bhosle to say they needed to check out the 'property card' for the house.

"What's that now?" Asked Shilpa, thinking Oh Christ another bloody complication.

"This is a card that shows legit ownership of the property. It has to have all the names of the people who claim to have a share in the property and has to be verified by the officers of the revenue department of the region. So we have to make sure that all the names of this family are on the card not just Roshan and mother," said Bhosle.

"This is more than I bargained for," said Shilpa to Jill after she put the phone down and then went on to explain to Jill the details.

Hours later she called Aspi to inform him that he needed to find out about the property card, also called PC. When he in turn asked Roshan she was surprised and not very helpful claiming she knew nothing about it. He then called the lawyer who had advised him earlier and was told to go to the Revenue office and check there. To his surprise neither his name nor that of any of the cousin were on the card except those who had passed away and those of Freny and Roshan after husband/father had died. When he asked what he needed to do Ravi said he had to prove he was Person of Indian Origin (PIO) and proof that he had claim to the property with death certificates and wills. This is going to be a bloody nightmare. It seems that PIO or OCI (Overseas Citizen of India) foreign passport holders can buy and sell property in India so long as it's not agricultural.

For the next two weeks Aspi and Armity sent letters and emails to all the relatives asking if they were PIOs and if they had copies of the wills and death certificates of the parents. It took all of two weeks to collect them with FedEx packages and certified mail envelopes crossing the oceans. Finally after three weeks all the files were ready and were taken to Ravi.

Their appointment was at 10 am but on arrival they were told that Ravi was going to be out all day be back tomorrow. The next day when they arrived he was with a man who seemed more like a friend than a man doing business. The two of them sat laughing and drinking tea while Aspi and Armity sat on a bench outside for over one hour.

When they finally entered Aspi placed a box of sweets in front of Ravi who dismissed it by calling his peon and handing it to him.

"You are from where?" Asked Ravi.

"We are Indian but now live in US and UK," replied Aspi.

"What passport you are having and you are PIO?"

"Yes we are. As you will see from the papers all these official and original papers show we are owners of the property with the person who is there now," said Aspi nervously and wiping his brow in the heat of the office.

"Ha, yes but this will is copy. I want original will. Why you bring this?"

"We only have the copies now and it's been years since our parents died. The death certs are originals."

Ravi went over them about four times and then said he will get back to them in a few days.

A month passed and then a letter came to Aspi saying their request had been rejected and their names could not get on to the card now. Depressed and frustrated he called Shalini who in turn called Bhosle. The three of them met at the Oberoi café. Shalini was edgy and testy so when Bhosle excused himself to go to the loo Aspi asked her "What's the matter you seem very distracted?"

"I am, my friend Jill is leaving early morning to get back to London and I need to be with her. I feel you should talk to Bhosle alone. Sorry I have to leave. See you soon."

When Bhosle retuned he explained the long and corrupt process in India and that what they will have to do is get a lawyer to make a case for them so there is no doubt as to why your name shouldn't be on the PC. Yes he was sorry that would be more expense but on the other side the sale would cover all this.

Aspi put his hands on his forehead and just shook it while his sister said she wanted to leave India and return to her family as this could take years.

When Shilpa reached her flat there was no sign of Jill. She asked the servants where 'Jill Madam' had gone and they said she had gone to Phoenix Mills mall to get some things. She tried to call her on the phone, as it had been over 3 hours since she left but no answer. When by 7 pm she had not returned Shilpa called the police but to no avail. They said there was nothing they could do but if she wasn't home tomorrow to call again. Frustrated she called her father who in turn called an old police friend and a private security company to look for Jill. Nothing- was the answer at 11 pm. Shilpa was besides herself and so were the servants who had really got to like Jill. It was three hours before the BA flight's take-off so Shilpa called the airline desk at the airport to ask if she had checked in by some fluke.

Ajit then had the thought of calling the police again near the mall and was told that there was someone, a foreigner, found in the ruins of the old mill near the mall but she was badly hurt and now in hospital in the area. Shilpa and Ajit went over to the hospital, dashed into the emergency only to be told family could see her. Ajit lost his temper and took out his cell phone and called a judge he knew. Within 10 minutes the judge called the hospital and Shilpa and Ajit were allowed to enter a room where Jill was tied down on a bed with bandages on her nose and head and the right arm in a sling but worst of all she was in a coma.

Shilpa was in a state of shock and had to be treated by the doctor and was laid down on the couch in Jill's room. Ajit sat there wondering what to do when a young man and girl walked in to ask how Jill was. It turned out that they were the couple that found Jill in the ruins of the mill.

"Sir, we just walking around spending the time together when we heard all these noises so we went to the darker part of the area and there three boys about 17 or so were raping this lady. I shouted and my friend Mangala took out her phone and called the police and then took some photos. I ran at them and threw stones and they ran away but madam was covered in blood and not in a modest state if you know what I mean," said the young man.

Then Mangala said, "She was very heavy bleeding sir. I tried to talk to her but she said she was attacked by these boys as they offered to get her to a taxi and then robbed her and then raping her and too much hitting her. Her nose was broken and her arm in very bad state."

Ajit thanked them and asked them to wait then called the police again via his friend the judge knowing they would react to him. It took over an hour for the Deputy commissioner and a Sargent to arrive. The couple went through their story and told the police that they lifted her up and got her into a taxi and brought her to the emergency at the hospital. They also showed the photos of the rape taken by Mangala, which the earlier police paid no attention to saying these foreigners ask for it. 'She probably tried to seduce the boys.'

Shilpa was zoned out at this stage after the injection the doctor gave her so wasn't in any state to respond but Ajit told the police he was going to report this to the press in the morning. The police insisted on taking the camera from the couple but Ajit insisted they transfer the photos to the computer from the phone and use that. They had no right to take the phone. This became an issue and then Ajit called the judge again and put the DC on the line. After about two minutes the DC took the phone over to the hospital computer so that the photos could be emailed to his site.

At 6.15 am a groan of anguish came from the bed, which woke up Ajit who had fallen asleep in the armchair. He alerted the nurse on duty and she in turn called the doctor who came running to see that Jill was conscious and asking for water. Shilpa woke up to the commotion and seeing Jill awake kissed her on the forehead. Ajit in turn called some friends in the press and asked the two people who had rescued Jill to come over in the morning.

Hours later when Mangala and her friend Sunder arrived there was a team of photographers and reporters to cover them and they were photographed standing on either side of Jill. Ajit asked them to come with him in his car which drove to the nearest ATM where he withdrew rupees 10,000 and gave each one 5,000. "Please do not forget to give a full account to the police and to the prosecution when the time comes and there will be another 5,000 for each of you then," said Ajit exchanging their names and addresses for the cash.

Shilpa then called the British High Commission and told them what had happened and that they should inform MI6 in London. A young doctor who over heard the call went and told one of the reporters about it. Next day in the Mirror, the tabloid that accompanies many main line papers, came the headline "James Bond girl raped in Mumbai." How the hell did that get out was the question at the High Commission.

When Jill started to recover and was able to speak she told her side of the story of how she was laden with bags and these young boys offered to help her get a cab. After they put her in the taxi they all bundled in and the driver shot off to the end of the ruins of the old mill where the boys pushed Jill out of the car and during the struggle hurt her arm and broke her nose. Then lifted her skirt and one after another forced themselves on her till the couple came to rescue her. She really didn't recall the details or their faces.

Jill asked to meet the young couple and had Shilpa cash four 100-Pound travellers checks and handed them both some cash. . Three days later a person from the High Commission came over to say they had arranged a passage for Jill on the next plane to London and she was to leave immediately, which she promptly did. Shilpa was in tears for the next 2 days.

24
IT NEVER ENDS

While Shilpa and her crew were doing their part in trying to sort out the 'heritage issue' and the sale of the property, Roshan was going around to the lower ranking clerks and throwing a spanner in the works. Her first attempt was to try to change the property card again but the clerk Ravi saw that there was no value in working with her and so told his colleagues to ignore her.

"The woman is a psycho yar, keeps bothering me every two three days" he told them. "These high minded Parsees have no idea how we work and survive. They live on trust funds and all that yar and likes of us have to work in these awful jobs and make ends meet. How we are going to do that if we can't make money on the side?" Asked Ravi.

A few days later Bhosle and Shilpa (aka Shalini) came to see Ravi with an envelope of the agreed price of Rupees 100,000. He opened the packet and actually counted the money in front of them saying, "Baas, only this?"

"But that's what we agreed to," said Bhosle.

"Come on yar, that woman psycho keeps coming every few days and wants me to do *hera-fera* for her but I said No. Look I have seen that property these people and you will make a fortune so come on be generous and make it 500,000 rupees," said Ravi with a smile.

"I can't believe this," said Shalini.

"Oh believe it dear," said Bhosle whispering, "these bastards are working us over and they know we can't do much and remember he has to pay his boss and the others below him too from all this loot."

Bhosle made a call to Ajit and it was agreed to give the clerk another 400,000 rupees or eight thousand US dollars.

Even after the payment was made the paper work wasn't done so the builder had to come back another day. "This is the problem in corrupt India compared with say China. There you also pay bribes but the work gets done. Here it's plain robbery!" said Bhosle to Shalini when they went out of the office.

When Roshan heard about the fact that changes were made to the card she confronted Aspi, "I will never forgive you for the rest of my life for what you have done to me!" she screamed at him as he entered the house. "Get out of the house now you are not welcome in it. Get out!"

Aspi was stunned and speechless then muttered, "Is this the way to speak to someone like your blood relative? I must remind you I have every right to this place as you do and I will stay as long as I want to. So if anyone has to leave you better go and don't ever talk to me like that again."

Roshan walked out of the room slamming the door behind her. Aspi just stood there in shock as Freny, Roshan's mother, walked into the room to ask what the shouting was about. Aspi, fuming inside of himself, just touched her on the shoulder and walked out of the house. He called Shalini/Shilpa and told her what had happened.

Shilpa heard what Aspi had to say but her mind was 6000 miles away thinking of Jill and how she missed her. It was 5.30 pm in India so 12-noon GMT so Shilpa called Jill at the office. Jill had been back at work for a week and it had been three weeks since she had left but the two women kept in touch every other day.

"Hi luv," said Jill.

"I miss you so much Jill. My body doesn't function, as it should, I look at my hands and wish your fingers were intertwined with mine. I miss everything about you. I can't believe I feel this way. Yesterday I bought some flowers and thought if I had a flower for every time I miss you in a day I wouldn't have room in my flat for them. Jill what are we going to do?" Asked Shilpa.

"I really don't know and this is all so strange for both of us. Did you ever think you would fall in love with a woman? I never even dreamt of it except as a schoolgirl when I was 'in love' with my English teacher, Miss Paulson, who was film star gorgeous. This is weird isn't it and yet so passionate and wonderful," said Jill.

"I will come to London soon. I promise," said Shilpa and they talked about what they were doing except Jill couldn't say much for obvious reasons and Shilpa understood.

"I had neglected my flower pots but the good thing in England is the constant rain and occasional shine so they are not too bad," said Jill.

"You are a wonderful gardener and you make my soul bloom when you touch me and talk to me. Oh I so wish I was in your arms right now," Shilpa's breathing got heavier and she had to sit down.

"I love you darling," said Jill and hung up the phone.

Bhosle and Shalini went to see Ravi the Revenue Clerk again three days later and they were working on the so called confession papers that the owners had to give for the family names to be changed. Ravi had three people writing out the several 'confessions' in Marathi by hand as they didn't know how to use the computer, which, was formatted for Marathi.

After waiting for two hours Aspi came to join Bhosle and Shalini and was told to get them some coffee from the local Café Coffee Day which he did and then insisted they translate these confessions to him in English. Now the reason for these documents is to establish that the genuine family members are offering them and that there is no objection to them by any of the other family members hence the many copies. To Aspi's shock and horror the clerks had got almost everything wrong and he refused to sign the papers. This meant another round of copying and as it was late they called it a day. "We will come back tomorrow to finish it," said Ravi.

The following day Bhosle called Ravi who told him that the papers couldn't be done, as they were required for urgent business so they had to wait again. Another two days went by and then one of the clerks named Sitaram told Ravi he wouldn't do the job for the pittance Ravi was giving him so Bhosle was asked to bring another 50,000 rupees for this man. Once again they sat down to do it and to their surprise in walked Roshan and told Ravi she had no faith in him or his team and that she was not going to sign the papers.

The words offended Ravi to the point that he told the clerks to put down their pens and forget the work. Just then Aspi who had heard from the house that Roshan had come to the Revenue office turned up and was told by Bhosle what had happened. He pleaded with Ravi to start the work and had to say his cousin was unstable and to forgive her outburst.

"I do this for you and Bhosle Seth only. You don't bring that Psycho Madam to me again. I will never do anything for her and nor will others in my office," said Ravi. Aspi nodded and shook his hand.

Finally the documents were done and Ravi decided to go through the reams of papers: the file was four inches thick. He insisted on all the original wills and death certificates.

"Sir please don't take the originals death certs as they are hard to get and we also don't have the original wills. Please accept the copies," pleaded Aspi.

Ravi put his pen down and looked at Bhosle and said in Marathi "Does he want the work done or not? If I want the originals then I want them tell him not to argue with me."

Bhosle explained the courts would want to see the originals so Aspi could get new ones by applying for them. As for the Xerox wills Ravi insisted on more money, as there were no originals.

"This is getting absurd!" called out Aspi. "When does this stop?"

Just then Shalini walked in to see how matters were progressing and was told by Roshan who was outside the office that this was a farce and that the work would never be done.

"Ravi what is going on?" She stormed into the office. "We have paid you all we have now get the fucking work done!"

Ravi slammed the pen down and walked out of the office. Bhosle shook his head and Aspi just dropped his head in his palms resting on his knees.

"Very good Shalini, very good. Now what we are to do?" Asked Bhosle.

"Break their fucking legs. I am sick of this ripping us off at every turn."

"My dear I am agreeing with you. You remember I told you how builders need to be successful?"

"Yes goons or as you call them goondas."

"Very good young lady. Time for the call."

Aspi escorted Roshan out of the office while Bhosle and Shalini got in a car and drove off. Aspi now had no idea what was going on but was a beaten man.

At 6 pm the sun was setting as Ravi walked out of his office with two of the three clerks. They were all laughing but it would be the last laugh they would have for a very long time.

Round the corner of the road four men jumped all three of them. They had scarves around their heads and faces. Two of them had cricket bats and the other two knuckle-dusters on their hands. In less than a minute they broke Ravi's legs and the knuckle-duster fists broke his nose. The other two were pushed to the ground and had their ribs kicked and a few unorthodox strokes played on their backs and legs with the bat. Quick as a flash the goondas jumped into a car that was already revved up and disappeared into the traffic. The rush hour crowd just stood and watched this display of brute aggression but did nothing about it.

Two days later Bhosle walked into Ravi's office to be told of the accident and that the man was still in hospital. He then walked to the other two men's desk in the open office and saw their sorry patched up faces and smiled.

"I heard what happened now are you going to do my work or not and who is in charge of signing the documents?" Asked Bhosle.

Within 30 minutes he had the papers in his hand and didn't bother to hand over the final envelope to the clerks who realised just who had beaten then up.

25
THE CIRCUS IS OVER

Roshan's face fell six blocks when Aspi waived the new property card in front of the cousin. A few hours later Ajit, Bhosle and Shalini walked into the drawing room and sat down to tea, sandwiches and cake.

"Well, Mr Aspi what are we talking about now for the price?" Asked Ajit.

"You make the offer first."

"Twenty-five crores or in your US money 5 million US dollars," said Ajit.

"You must be joking," said Aspi.

"You are bloody mad!" Said Roshan who knew flats were going for that sum so a bungalow with almost an acre of ground had to be worth double.

Ajit sipped his tea and then went into the trouble they had getting all the work done but that didn't move either Aspi or Roshan.

"Think on it and we will return in a day or so," said Bhosle and they all got up and walked out.

Aspi wanted to get back and close the deal so he called Shalini three days after the walk out and said they would settle on forty crores or US dollars eight million. Shalini drove over and spoke to the cousins for half an hour to convince them to take thirty five and that the buyer would pay all the legal fees and stamp papers but not the capital gains tax and they could not be held responsible for any family quarrels. Emails and faxes were sent out to all the other relatives and within 48 hours they had their reply: Sell, sell, and sell!

Roshan was losing a lot of her hair now due to stress and found she was screaming at people especially the servants and her cousin who had come to the conclusion she was heading for a nervous breakdown. She simply wanted the house and no one else would get it. When Aspi walked into the house with the draft of the deal Roshan flipped and screamed at Aspi to get out of the house. Aspi left to see a lawyer.

The lawyer's office was on Sir Phiroshah Mehta road where many of the old Parsee lawyers and stockbrokers sit today. In their days these magnificent buildings were the pride of Bombay but in this time of Mumbai they have become decrepit and disgustingly dirty. Even the rich lawyers couldn't be bothered to paint or clean them as all they are interested in is making money and paying their clerks low wages. Some of them in 2009 still use old Remington typewriters and carbon paper. The most disgusting part of the offices are the shared toilets. It's better to wait and relieve yourself at home or go to a five star hotel.

One such lawyer was a 78 year old Pestonji Wadia who the Dorabjee family had used over the years but he should have retired 8 years ago, sadly with no wife or children, he kept the office going with his 64 year old secretary Themina and 56 year old clerk, Joshi, who had been with him for over 25 years and neither wanted to learn this new contraption called a computer or fax machine. They still sent telegrams and typed on the old manual machine.

Aspi found it difficult to deal with these people. First their slowness and second they didn't revert back to him but insisted on calling Roshan which irritated him a lot. After very little was achieved he took matters in his own hand and sacked Wadia and went to a smart young lawyer called Roy Modi who had an international practice in Hong Kong and Singapore.

Within a month the work was done. Advertisements were put in English papers in case there was any objection to say the land was being sold. Measurements of the land was done by the buyers and the whole process to change the names on the property card had to be redone with Rs. 10 lakhs, $10,000, being passed over the table for the clerk. All this took 6 weeks and the final deal to be signed was to be done at the lawyer's office. The family arrived ten minutes early except Roshan.

"Where the hell is that woman?" yelled Aspi. "She is out to screw this up as much as she can. I will bloody sue her sari and choli off her!!"

The lawyer and the family waited for 40 minutes and that's when one of the families from the USA said, "Lets sign our names and then get it over with after all we have the majority."

"Ah, but is the will probated for the majority clause to be activated?" asked the junior lawyer.

People shrugged their shoulder. Within a minute Roshan rushed in waving a paper saying "It's not probated and I will not sign and you majority have no hold on the property. So you can all go to hell!"

"Wills can take ages to get activated in probate court but we can fast track it if you are willing to pay for it? Asked Modi.

They all nodded except Roshan.

Leave it to me said Modi and you all comeback tomorrow.

The next morning Modi took the will to the 'clerk of wills' and was told the man could not help as a lady 'Madam Roshan' had called and said nothing was to be touched she was the main owner of the bungalow and the cousins were cheating her. "She has been here many times Modi Sahib and we call her Psycho Madam. What rubbish she talking sir but she is bringing court order so vat to do sir?" Said the clerk.

"Bloody bitch!" yelled Modi banging on the table. "Help me and I will help you. Come on we have known each other for years. What will it take?" He took a wallet out of his inside pocket and pulled out 5 one thousand-rupee bills.

"What sir those days are over. Today if you want to lose Psycho Madam's notice then help me with 25,000. I too have a house to run and pay school fees," said the thin clerk whose fingers were covered in ink and his teeth were rotten chewing tobacco but mainly what disgusted Modi was the BO, it looked like his shirt hadn't touched water for days just a lot of hot sweat.

Modi wasn't carrying that sort of cash on him so he left to go to an ATM and get another 20,000 to pay this bastard. The clerk took the crisp 25 notes and looked over his shoulder and stuffed them into his back pocket. Modi waited in the hot room for over ninety minutes then the clerk came out with a more senior man and said the deal was not possible because he said this madam was "too much powerful lady,"

"You are joking sir," said Modi and immediately took out his cell phone and called the judge he knew in the high court. It took him five minutes to explain the situation and then handed the cell over to the senior Babu whose face went ashen and he handed the phone back to the lawyers saying to the junior clerk "Do whatever he wants and then go home."

When Modi and Aspi took the new will with all the correct probate stamps on it there was a verbal explosion at the house. Roshan started to scream. "Get out of the house."

"Get out of my house you fucking bastards from America. You have come to ruin my happiness." She threw the will on the sofa and walked out of the room yelling at the men.

Within minutes of the drama the phone rang and it was one of the cousins from the UK who asked if the house was sold and if so what was her share? Aspi said "This is it we are going to sell it on majority vote."

The next morning the team of Shilpa and Ajit More came to the property accompanied by 2 lawyers and an accountant. They made themselves comfortable at the table and handed over 4 cheques of five crores each. Then opened 2 briefcases next to the accountant who then counted 10 crores in used notes of 50, 100, 500 and 1000. They divided the notes between them and counted them on the large queen size bed for over 2 hours. Yes, the 30 crores were there, now to be divided between the family.

Aspi and Modi took a deep breath at seeing the thousands of notes laid out in neat bundles when Roshan rushed in and swept the piles of notes on to the floor in one swoop of the hand and then banged on the bed till almost all the notes were on the floor. She then called out to the houseboy to come and pick up the notes and take them away.

"Enough is enough you bloody bitch!" yelled Aspi and slapped Roshan across the face and then hammered the other cheek with a backhand. He always had a good tennis backhand. "Don't pick her up or you too will get it from me," yelled Aspi to the servant. The old retainer helped collect the notes slipping the odd one into his pocket and they finally cleared the room. When they walked out Roshan was heard crying on the floor. Finally beaten or was she?

Over the next few hours the lawyers and the accountants sat and worked out the shares. Finally three hours later the shares were completed and the agents got their share of 10% plus their expenses for all the work that had been done. Shilpa and her dad's company walked away with 3 crores about $500,000 in US dollars.

Ajit gave his daughter one crore and told her to get out of India and find some happiness even if it was with Jill in London. "Go daughter find someone to love and be loved. Remember in the bible Ruth loved Naomi-these people are so hypocritical that they forget their own good book when it comes to matters they don't like. It's not a matter of whom you love but the fact that you really love someone that matters to you. Go to London and find Jill if not Tito and for God sake live and be loved by them for the rest of your life."

Shilpa poured a glass of Glen Grant for both of them, Ajit leant back on the recliner and took a long swig of the single malt and then gave small cry and took a deep breath. Shilpa turned to see what was wrong but noticed the glass on the rug and saw Ajit's head on one side and his tongue hanging out of his mouth. It was all over for Ajit More.

His death made all the 24/7 news channels and the front page of all the major papers. The funeral was delayed by a day as they realised thousands would attend-not so much for Ajit More but to be seen in public and be photographed for page 3 of the dailies.

The circus over, Shilpa caught a first class flight on Virgin to LHR to see her two closest friends Tito and Jill.

26
THE TIGRESS IN LONDON

The Taj Group of Indian hotels owns the St. James Court Hotel and as Ajit had a lot of influence with them he was able to get Shilpa a good rate. It's a fine five-star hotel, which is in walking distance of Buckingham Palace advertises a spa and a one star Michelin gourmet restaurant.

Shilpa stood at the window overlooking the courtyard with a gushing fountain and verdure. The door opened behind her and she felt the presence of a person. She turned around slowly to see Jill standing there, but she didn't move till Jill walked towards her and she leapt at her and bit her neck, then kissed her cheeks passionately and finally placed her lips on her mouth and they stayed locked in that position for what seemed like eternity. Finally Shilpa pulled back and looked at Jill who was in tears. "I have missed you so much I can't even speak about it," said Jill.

"You mean everything to me. What you make me feel nothing else matters and I don't give a damn what the world thinks of us. I love you so much Jill," said Shilpa and kissed her again and again. Within a minute both women were naked on the bed ferociously devouring every erotic moment they could from the encounter.

The following morning they both sat in front of the window eating breakfast in the white hotel bathrobes. "You know they make these fabulous Turkish towel robes in India but you can't buy them there. Isn't it absurd!" said Shilpa. Jill smiled she was thinking, what on earth am I going to do with her? What am I doing here?

For the next several days' life just drifted in those last days of summer for Shilpa and Jill. They walked in the park across from the hotel, licking each other's ice-cream cones, lying in the grass with hundreds of others soaking in the sun. Shilpa seemed at peace for the very first time in her life but not Jill; she was like a volcano inside wanting to erupt but still the lava was boiling and had not reach its peak to explode.

A week into their first encounter at the hotel Shilpa said "I have fallen in love for the first time in my life because you bring stability and emotional security to what was once a vicious, selfish and arrogant woman. You are so secure in whom you are and that translates into my life and makes me at peace with myself. Do I make sense to you?" Asked Shilpa.

"Shilpa I have no idea what I am doing. No I am not secure as you put it just the reverse. Yesterday I took your framed picture on my bookshelf and threw it out of the window hoping it would help me get rid of you inside of me. It didn't, then I wanted to write an email but that would be cowardly and you would storm into my office, I know you. Finally here I am telling you I need to break this off it's just not right for me. I have a life at the office and that's all I have and they won't like you being in mine. I love you so much that it really hurts," said Jill

"I love you so much too and I can't imagine my life without you. I have been so happy for the first time in my life these past few days since coming back from India. Please don't do this," said Shilpa crying.

"For a time you will be hurt, then sad and mourn, but slowly the healing will begin when one day you will wake up and say −What the hell was all that about anyway!"

Shilpa looked at Jill wanting to hold her but instead turned and walked towards the hotel without ever turning back. Jill watched her walk away and hoped she would turn back but when she didn't she too walked to the tube station to go home.

The ITN 10'oclock news was on but Shilpa's mind was not on the troubles around the globe when suddenly the phone ringing shook her. "Hi, I know you would call. Thank God that was all so silly," said Shilpa.

"Really you thought I would call?" Said a man's voice.

"Who is this?"

"Who do you think? It's me Tito. Who were you hoping for?"

"Oh My God Tito how did you know I was here?"

"Darling I am still on the books of the office and we know you have been here for some time now and that you have been with Jill. Don't worry so long as it's nothing to do with work then no one cares these days but I care for you as I always have. To be honest Jill called me a few minutes ago and she was concerned about you," said Tito.

"Oh really. Funny way of showing it that's for sure," replied Shilpa.

"Would you like me to come over?

"No not tonight but try me tomorrow may be some company will be good for me. This is a new experience being dumped like this just when I thought I had found the love of my life," said Shilpa holding back her tears and then finally burst out crying.

She heard the phone click on the other end. "I need to take a pill and sleep. May be two tonight," She said loudly to herself.

27
SHE MUST RETURN

L ondon has a population of over 10 million and yet Shilpa was so very lonely. She couldn't stop thinking of Jill, her slim body, the long legs, the mango shaped breasts but most of all the wide lips that people often said she had a "Botox job" but she hadn't just natural lush red lips.

Shilpa tried to meet other women and men. She rode horses in Hyde Park, went to the Dorchester for tea hoping to make eye contact with someone. She even tried to meet people on the Internet but after 3 dates she gave that up. One of them happened with a transvestite who hadn't had the full operation and was shocked when he-she whipped out her 8 inch muscle to excite Shilpa who in turn pulled up her panties and with bra in hand ran out into the street. This wasn't working for sure.

Two months after she had last seen Jill she decided to ring on her front door and see if she could talk to her. When the door opened a man stood there and said

"Hello. Can I help you?"

"No sorry it's the wrong flat. I was looking for Jill," said Shilpa

"Darling there is a lady here looking for you," shouted the man.

Jill appeared over his broad shoulders. "My God what are you doing here at this time?"

"Sorry, really sorry I thought you might be alone and wanted to talk to you. I miss you so much."

The man looked at Jill and said, "Is this the famous Shilpa? I must say you are as stunning as Jill described you. Look she and I are an item now and I must ask you to leave-please," said the man politely but Shilpa didn't move and just stared at Jill.

"Shilpa this is Derek and he and I are now seeing each other. Sorry but I think its best you go," said Jill gently.

Shilpa stared at the couple and without a word went down the stairs; she got in her car, opened a pack of gum and waited. The wait went on for three hours and finally at 1 am she saw the front door open and Derek came down the stairs and got into his VW Jetta and drove off.

Shilpa saw Jill drawing the curtains for the night and the light in her bedroom went off. Just then she saw a resident coming up the stairs so she rushed out of the car with her French beret on and driving gloves still covering her hands and followed the resident into the foyer but didn't get in the lift with him but bounced up the stairs.

She looked to see if anyone was on Jill's landing and then rang her bell. It took a couple of minutes for the door to open and Jill said, "So what did you forget…. Oh my God don't stalk me Shilpa please."

Shilpa forced herself into the room. She held Jill's face with her gloved hands and kissed her passionately. For a moment Jill responded and then pushed Shilpa away.

"This nonsense has to stop. Now!!" yelled Jill.

"I can't you are my life, my all. Everything around me reminds me of you, the sound of rain, the smell of Ferragamo perfume, when someone touches my hand I want it to be yours. I dream of you every single night… Come back to me please!"

Jill saw the tears in Shilpa's eyes and touched her face gently then her knee and that aroused Shilpa whose hand moved under Jill's kimono and started to stroke her thigh, this made Jill take a deep breath and come forward to kiss Shilpa.

Shilpa pushed Jill's chair to the floor then mounted her and the two women started tearing the clothes off each other. As the two naked bodies rubbed against each other Shilpa called out, "Now tell me that you don't love me, tell me! I love you so much I want you for the rest of my life!"

Jill pushed Shilpa's body over to the side and tried to sit up. "I will always care for you but I need to have a normal life and home and maybe Derek can provide that," said Jill.

Shilpa jumped back on to Jill's body and held her throat gently at first and then the grip got tighter and harder with Jill kicking and trying to scream but no sound was being uttered. Shilpa reached for the sofa cushion and covered Jill's face while her body flayed, her arms and legs moving frantically for 3 minutes and then suddenly sagged to the floor.

Seeing there was no blood on the cushion, Shilpa stood up and looked down on the dead body. She lifted Jill's head and coolly banged it against the edge of the sofa and buried the face in the thick Persian carpet. Picking up the pillow she went around the room wiping up what could be seen as evidence re a murder in the room. It was now 2 am, she slowly opened the front door and seeing the passage empty she walked to the incinerator shoot and pushed the cushion down. Then took a tea cloth and wiped the place clean except where she saw bottles and glassed that Jill and Derek must have used.

She used the stairs to go down as she saw the lift was in use. Her car took off from 0 to 60 in 10 seconds. She drove down Drayton Gardens into the Fulham road; up to Kensington High Street and from there she went home the very long way.

At MI6 no one questioned Jill's absence the next day or the day after. These days life was slow and people took odd days off. Shilpa went to Lloyds Bank and asked to withdraw all 600,000 Pounds and have them transferred to a Swiss account that she had spent days arranging before she met Jill. It was time to go and go far away. Never to see emerald shores of England, well certainly for a few years.

Three days after Jill's absence from the MI6 office the Director asked her co-workers to look into her absence. Calls were made to her house and then when no answer came all day. Her colleague Mark Temple went over to the flat in Drayton Court but found the door locked and no answer. He went to the building supervisor and using his credentials got him to open Jill's door.

"Oh my God what's that bloody smell?" Called out Mark.

"Jesus Christ, its bad news," said the Irish building super. "Smells like a dead body."

They entered the living room to find a blue coloured Jill laid out on the floor with dried blood around her head and on the corner of the chair near her.

"Don't touch a thing," said Mark. He took out his cell phone and called the boss at the office.

Twenty minutes later came the local Metropolitan police, MI5 and the Director. The medical officer from the Met examined the body for 20 minutes and worked out she had been dead for at least three to four days- body was decomposing rapidly in the central heating of the flat. Several of the cops and the MI6 team put Vicks in their nostrils to keep the stench away.

"Who was she associated with?" asked the MI5 man to the Director. "Are we to treat this as a terrorist action?'

"I don't have an answer right now, not a clue," said the Director. "Never knew her to have any terrorist enemies. I mean in our line of work like yours we meet the scum of the earth but she wasn't involved personally in any case that I know of where someone would kill her. Wonderful person and loved by all at the office."

"Well I guess we will have to work together and with the Met. God knows what they will come up with. Don't want them botching up any of our trails to other people," said the man from MI5.

"Quite so," said the Director and walked out of the room beckoning to Mark to leave as well.

At St. Pancras station Shilpa was boarding the Channel train to Paris. Little over two hour later she was at Gare du Nord in the centre of the city. From there she took a taxi to Rue Chateaubriand just off the Champs Elysees. There she booked into a small hotel with her old MI6 passport and went upstairs to her room. She unpacked and took a pair of scissors and cut her hair above her shoulders, mixed a brown dye and highlighted her black hair. She changed from her pantsuit into a black mini skirt and white top, put on her two-inch pumps and repacked her bag.

Shilpa tried to watch the TV for a while but the prime time French talk shows bored her. She tuned into the BBC World News but there was nothing about a murder or death of a MI6 agent. Time past slowly, at 2 am she took her large bag down the lift and asked the sleepy night porter to get a cab. He wandered out and whistled for a Citroen taxi to draw up, put her bag in the back and accepted a small tip.

"Do you speak English?" Asked Shilpa.

"Oui, why not," replied the African driver.

"OK I want you to drive me to Lyon tonight can you do that?"

"For 500 Euros I do anything."

"Five hundred you must be joking! I will give you two hundred and if you drive fast another hundred. That's more than you make in 2 days. If you can't let me out near the nearest taxi stand," said Shilpa sharply.

"OK, OK, I go, you hard woman madam."

Normally the 460 km journey takes over four hours but the way the African drove to get his big tip they reached the cathedral in just over three hours dealing with the trucks on the night road.

Shilpa asked him to drop her at an all-night café. It was now after 5 am, chilly and hungry she ordered a hot soup and some cheese and bread. What should she do now? Plan had come to a halt.

At the Kensington police station the homicide detectives were scratching their heads. No clues at all. They had finger printed the place; found Jill's prints and couple of others with no match in their computers. They spoke to Mark and the

Director but were told Jill kept her private life very private but may be Tito a freelance officer of the office may know more.

Tito was woken out of bed after midnight by a ring on his door. The woman in his bed shot up revealing her naked body but Tito took no notice, turned over and went to sleep.

More rings and knocking.

"Who the hell is it?" yelled Tito walking towards the door.

"Metropolitan Police, please open up sir"

The door opened and inch and Tito saw the badge flashed in front of his droopy face.

"Want some coffee. I need it if you don't," said Tito going to the kitchen and taking out three mugs and heating the water.

The cops stood in the kitchen and told him they were there to ask him about Jill.

Forty minutes later they left having learnt about Jill's boyfriend, Shilpa and her affair with Jill and his affair with Shilpa. Tito was not the most loyal of friends when it came to saving his own skin and job.

"Listen Harry," said Chief Inspector Watson to his detective inspector Harry Baines "Look up the boyfriend and see if you can get that Indian woman Shilpa to cooperate. Get her to come to the station for a chat. Don't scare them or make any threats. Maybe something there but who knows."

By the next morning they had traced Derek and he was in the interview room where he told them all he knew about the last time he met Jill and about this woman called Shilpa who had a crush on Jill.

"Bloody lesbo bitch I bet she killed her. Go after her," said Derek.

Watson and Baines found Shilpa had left her flat a week ago and no one knew where she was. "What do you recon Gov.?" asked Baines.

"Bank accounts. Track down her account and speak to the manager."

It took a day to track her account at the Lloyds branch. There are several Shilpa Morays in the Indian community. Baines walked into the manager's office and asked about Shilpa Moray account.

"She left us some time ago. Took all her money out and transferred it to Zurich. Can't tell you anymore," said the manager.

"You can, for a start which bank did she transfer it to?"

"We'll all I know it was a number and the transfer was done on a routing number so it could be any one of a dozen banks in Zurich. I am sorry but that all I can say. Give you the number if you like," said the manager trying to be helpful.

The next day Watson was on the phone to a M. Olivetti at a small bank in Zurich.

"Sir, please understand I am investigating a murder not a bank fraud. Now please cooperate and tell me if a Shilpa Moray transferred over five hundred thousand Pounds to you some ten days ago?"

"Sir you understand I am a Swiss banker and I have to tell you nothing. Now you listen I don't care if this person blew up Buckingham Palace I still say nothing. This is why people invest their money in Swiss banks. Good-bye," Olivetti slammed the phone down.

"Bloody Swiss we should have taken them over after the war. Bastards hid all that Nazi money and who knows what else."

Watson stubbed out his cigarette and opened his bottom draw and took a swig out of the Teachers whisky he kept hidden.

28
ZURICH

Shilpa walked out of the B&B where she was staying in Lyon, telling folks she was working on a project to do with the history of French cuisine. It gave her an excuse to go to all the small restaurants but to stay away from the three star ones. What should she do?

She called Olivetti in Zurich to hear that the British police had enquired about her. Her heart skipped a beat and her stomach churned.

"Don't worry madam you are in safe hands with our bank. We are not interested in any one's personal life. Do you want I should send money to you now?" Asked Olivetti.

"No I am alright just now thank you. I would like you to book me in a hotel in Zurich for tomorrow in the name of the bank and I will settle with you when we meet, please," said Shilpa.

"Done, it's no problem. You and your father are very loyal to the bank. How is he now?'

"He died some time ago," said Shilpa whose eyes brimmed up with tears.

"I am really sorry to hear that. He was one of my very first customers so I will always remember him. Miss Shilpa the bank will be honoured to host you in Zurich. Come safely."

She used cash all the way so there was no trace of credit cards.

Within 24 hours Shilpa was on a train to the Swiss border. There she ordered a taxi to take her to Zurich and to the Swiss-Italian bank where Olivetti greeted her like a lost daughter.

She told him she was getting away from a love affair with a man who was hounding her but as for his so-called murder enquiry she knew nothing.

"Who was murdered Senor Olivetti?"

"I have no idea Miss Shilpa but they were asking about money you transferred from London. But you know our mouth is like our safes no one can break in," said Olivetti with a smile.

He took Shilpa out to a lakeside bistro and then accompanied her to the hotel.

Olivetti was a slim man just under six feet, he had turned 50 just a few weeks ago, with salt-pepper hair, which flowed over his ears, he looked older. His northern Italian Renaissance features appealed to Shilpa; she had never cared about people's ages anyway.

After the porter put down the bag and offered to bring up some coffee Olivetti turned to Shilpa and asked if she would like a massage.

"Oh yes please. Can you ask the girl to come up in thirty minutes please?"

"Well I don't have to, you see my dear I am pretty damn good as the Americans say. I am serious I will put you to sleep in twenty minutes. I suggest you take a hot shower and then have some green tea and I will take over."

Olivetti ordered the green tea and coffee for himself. Shilpa saw herself in the large bathroom mirror and was shocked to see her new self with the short hair and streaks but she also looked very tired and stressed. What the hell if he wants to have me it may relax me and I need a good rogering.

She wrapped herself in a towel and was dripping on the carpet when she saw Olivetti in shirtsleeves and ready for his offer to put her to sleep. She drank the green tea called 'Sleepy time' and then without a word took off her towel and lay on the bed with her bare back facing Olivetti.

He took the body lotion from the bathroom and started to rub her back and then her legs and finally her feet; all the time in disbelief that this gorgeous woman had simply stripped in front of him within 4 hours of their first meeting. How he wanted to caress the body and make love to her! But Shilpa fell fast asleep and he was too much of a gentleman to disturb her. So he covered her with the duvet and left the room.

"Harry I just got word that Indian bitch went off to Paris on Ryan Air but there is no trace of her after that. See what you can find out," said Watson to Baines.

"She could be in bloody Timbuktu for all we know. Assuming that Jill woman had been dead for three days it's now over two weeks since then. I was also a bit surprised that she had died of asphyxiation. There is no evidence of anything there to say she didn't die from that fall and hit the chair."

"Well according to the coroner report she was killed by both smothering and the knock on the head. There must have been a fight. No other signs but the place was clean unless the killer really had time to wipe the place down and then get out. Looks to me like a pro job not something a jealous lover would do. What think you?" Asked Watson.

"Well you never know with these spooks. I think it was a hit from someone she was after. The girlfriend thing is just a wild goose chase. She was just pissed off and left the country. Let the MI5 sort it out its in their court with MI6. I know they hate each other. May be the MI5 knocked her off," laughed Baines.

"Not so fast Harry. I still have a feeling for this bird. She is like a humming bird; once they take off they don't stop till they get to their next habitat. Yes she is flying somewhere," said Watson pondering over a map of the world.

"Harry you ever been to India? Well we are going there mate. I'll get clearance so get ready to leave in 2 days."

———❖❖❖———

Zurich is Switzerland's largest city with a population of almost two million. Its history goes back to the Romans but early settlements have been found going back 6400 years making it one of Europe's oldest cities and now one of the world's premiere financial centres; Its rich in art and music and the home of one of the most important German speaking theatres in Europe.

"Shilpa why don't you settle here. I can get you a new identity and no one will ever bother you. I would personally like to take care of you if you so wish," said Olivetti as he held her hand over dinner, just two days after she had arrived.

"Oly, isn't that what people call you? I am amazed you said this to me I have known you for 48 hours. Are you serious?

"I have never been more serious Shilpa I saw you naked and I could have taken advantage yesterday but I said I respect this woman too much and maybe I can even love her. Oh Darling voglio baciare e appassionato amore adesso," said Olivetti, in his best Marcello Mastroianni voice, then leaned over the small table and kissed Shilpa gently on the cheek.

"You are very sweet but if I saw you naked I would probably die laughing," said Shilpa giggling. "You know Oly don't try to get women with talk because women know words better than men. We want to see action and not some caveman act, well sometimes even that works, but action my dear bank manager."

In his brain her lips touched his lips and a warm glow spread through his body. I love this woman he said to himself as a gypsy selling roses walked up to the table. He took the entire bunch of 15 roses and put 20 Euros in her hand and then spread them out in front of Shilpa.

She smiled, "You are moving on the right track but not there yet Mr Banker."

They sat looking at the lake and listening to the trio playing Strauss waltzes- No words were needed- Silence can be golden.

Two hours later his lips hovered over hers in the hotel room. His right arm floated over her legs and as their lips met his hands touch her thigh.

"Now my dear good girl starts to be bad. I mean very bad. Ti adaro," whispered Oly.

"If you are looking for sensitive love and understanding then go see a shrink but if you want some wild sex get those Gucci loafers off and fuck my brain out."

In seconds the loafers, trousers and shirt came off and he pulled Shilpa's dress over her head and noted she didn't wear a bra. He buried his face between her tits and bit the firm brown nipples. Suddenly for Shilpa the past was over, well for those few minutes, she had forgotten what it was like to be touched by a man. It's not bliss its sheer ecstasy.

29
THE CHASE

The case was now bigger than expected and the trail to India seemed worthwhile.

The plane from London landed at Mumbai airport building. It was still not what it should be for a world-class international airport but there was talk of yet another new terminal to open in 2014, which was still four years away. The CBI who had been alerted by Scotland Yard met Watson and Baines.

The flight had got in around midnight so the two cops decided to rest up in the hotel and then meet the regional head of the CBI.

"I am sorry to tell you people but this case of Shilpa More is closed in our files now. I have asked a person who was attached to her case many years ago to meet us but now please enjoy good Indian chai while we wait for him," said the Special Director of the CBI.

Couple of cups of tea later in walked a person Shilpa would have been shocked to see, now Deputy Commissioner Dinsoo Dubash who back in 1998 had been a sub inspector with the Mumbai police then attached to the Shilpa case.

Dubash was a wealth of information about the Shilpa Moray he knew but seeing the photograph he was handed by the Brits he said, "Gentleman this is not our Shilpa. She may have some looks close to her but not our girl. Our Shilpa escaped from here and years later we found out that the Taliban in Afghanistan had kidnapped her. That was the last of her. Sorry you have wasted your trip."

"Are you sure sir this isn't the same girl? This girl worked for a while for CNC and our own MI6," said Watson.

"Hundred and one per cent Chief Inspector. We may have photo of our Shilpa but you will see this is not she. She was kidnapped and escaped with the help of the CIA back in 1998 and we had to eat humble pie you might say and cover up the goof-up. You must know Shilpa More is a common name in this part of the world." Dubash shook hands and walked out shaking his head and thinking —my God who would have thought that case would come back 12 years later.

Back in London the two detectives entered the office of the Director of MI6.

"Sorry sir but we drew a blank in India. Seems this girl was captured by the Taliban and no mention has been made of her since 1998," said Watson.

The Director smiled to himself and thought we can't go any further than this. Let's close the case for now.

"Gentlemen thank you, sorry you had a wild goose chase but did you get to see Bombay? I was posted there at the consulate in the 60s."

"Yes the Indians are very hospitable and took us around in a car they build called an Ambassador which is our 1956 Morris Oxford and as for the traffic, unbelievable! I could never drive there," said Baines.

They were offered the customary sherry but refused it and left the Director pondering about his people and Shilpa in particular.

Zurich was getting cold in December and Shilpa was getting bored with Oly even though they were known as an item now and moved in very high circles. On a Thursday afternoon her cell phone rang.

"Don't say a word just come to my office at once please," said Oly.

Her heart jumped and she walked fast crossing the tram tracks and ran up the steps of the bank building.

"What is it? Why so secretive? Asked Shilpa.

Olivetti put his finger to his lips and pointed to the door across from the office.

"I have Scotland Yard here and MI6 from London they want to talk to you. Now I have said nothing but they know we are a couple, so to speak, so don't lie about that. It's about that murder but I don't know much more. Please be careful darling."

Shilpa walked into the next office to find Mark and another man sitting there. She nodded to Mark who she knew slightly and the other man got up to introduce himself as Commander Ian Fawn. Greying at the temples, medium height, she guessed he was in his forties.

"Ms. Shilpa Moray I presume?" he said putting out his hand. "I believe you know Mark Temple from the firm we are here to ask some questions and clear up a mystery is that OK with you?"

"Sure what can I do for you?" Her heart rate doubled in two seconds.

They went into her relationship with Jill, about what happened the last time they met and how Derek asked her to leave the flat, it went on and on, over and over again for two hours.

"Please I am in shock can't you see. I can't believe my Jill is dead. You need to leave me alone. I just can't go on," cried Shilpa.

Olivetti walked in as he had been listening, the whole time, via a microphone in the boardroom, which, he as the MD had placed in his office, so he could hear the board discuss issues behind his back. "Gentlemen you have been with Ms. Moray a long time and as her guardian, you might say, I have to make sure she is not too distressed and she looks very upset right now," said Olivetti in a calm but firm tone.

The two men said nothing but good-bye and left the office.

"Shilpa you are not safe here anymore. They can't deport you without a strong case but I fear for you. Now darling I want to know the truth and the whole truth about this Jill and you. So start at the beginning and bring me up to date," said Olivetti.

Over the next hour Shilpa told the condensed version of her life and Olivetti didn't say a word. What she left out were some of the dramas before she was taken by the Taliban and of course the killing of Jill. She saw Jill the last time with Derek and she was so upset that she wanted to leave the country for ever and hence she was in Zurich and happy to be with Oly.

"I am scared for you and these people are ruthless if they want to get you they will and I fear I will find you dead in a dark alley one night," said Oly.

Over the next few hours Shilpa was stunned, overwhelmed with fear and the chance of going to jail again was not an option. Life has to be better than this and I am not a spring chicken any more, she thought. Her life flashed in front of her and she knew there was no way she could take any more pain. Both Olivetti and she were staring at the world map on his office wall when her eyes focused on the islands of the south Pacific. She walked up to the map and pointed.

"That's where I am going and you can send me the money as and when I need it and you can even come over during the winter months to be with me."

"Tonga?"

"Yes no one will believe I will ever go there and I will be away from all this and with my money I can buy a citizenship of the island and then travel with a new name and passport," said Shilpa with a smile.

The next day the MI6 and Scotland Yard arrived to speak to Olivetti only to find he had left in the morning for Rome and as for Ms. Moray no one had any idea. Oh no thought Mark not another bloody chase. "You know Ian we don't have a damn thing on her and this chasing around is a waste of tax payer's money. What do you say?" Asked Mark. Ian nodded but he had his doubts.

There was something about this woman but they just couldn't pin it on her. May be MI6 will deal with her in time. So without a word got he got into the rental car and drove back to the airport and flew to London.

39,500 feet in the air Shilpa was relaxing on her flight to Sidney and from there on a cruise to the south Pacific. Oly had booked her out of Milan where they had driven overnight and taken the Qantas flight via Singapore. Clever Oly had her disembark at Singapore and then stay overnight at the airport hotel and take the Singapore Air flight to Sidney, joined a cruise line there the next day and sailed into the sunset to Tonga but in all this time she never gave a thought for Jill.

30
THE ESCAPE

Tonga became known as the 'Friendly Islands' because of the congenial reception accorded to the great sea -explorer Captain James Cook on his first visit in 1773. He arrived at the time of the *'inasi* festival, the yearly donation of the First Fruits to the Tu'i Tonga (the islands' paramount chief) and so received an invitation to the festivities.

In recent years it's had a constitutional monarchy and in 2010 when Shilpa went there it was King George Tapou V who was the ruler. On seeing Shilpa at a local casino he asked for her to be invited to the palace.

"Are you visiting or doing a research paper miss?" Asked the King.

"No your majesty I am hoping to make Tonga my home. I have travelled the world and it seems that Tonga is the place for me. Away from wars and back stabbing people. I want a life of serenity and a chance to watch good satellite TV and eat and get fat so your majesty will fancy me as one of your queens!"

They both laughed aloud, but people were jealous that this brazen hussy was taking their kings affections. When she got back to the hotel a large scattering of roses were spread across the bed and a note: *Tomorrow night, my lovely, it will be my bed-the king.*

Here we go again but well talking to a king is better than a Swiss banker or a Afghan general or even a screwing an Indian film star. I wish it were Darius or Jill. I am a fool but I survive.

Under the king's orders she was taken to the office of the citizenship and within 49 minutes a passport appeared but Shilpa spent over 100,000 Pounds between the bribes and the so-called Passport fees. She was now officially a Tonga lady. In her slim figure wearing a light brown silk dress that fell so flowingly to the ground, she drove up to the palace gates where she was escorted to the reception room; there welcomed by a young woman in a sarong who took her by the hand leading her into a room with a four poster bed which had roses and orchids scattered all over it. The young girl left and Shilpa sat on the bed awaiting "the royal entry."

After about five minutes the door opened and a large man with a very large stomach arrived and smiled at the maiden on the bed.

"You know if I could put the English alphabet together I would put I and U next to each other," said the fat man with a lecherous smile.

"Really if I could rearrange the alphabet I would put F and U together. Who the hell are you? I have come to see the King," said Shilpa sharply.

The fat man laughed like this was the best joke he had heard. "You are funny lady. I think you are very special I would die for you."

"OK then prove it!" snapped back Shilpa.

"I am general Tommy, the kings cousin, I know how to please a woman," said the general

"Then please leave me alone and let me go home that would please me."

"I am thinking of you all day after I saw you with the king yesterday. Who do you think arranged all this for you and sent you roses? No not His Majesty it was I. Let me give myself to you," begged the general.

"Sorry but I don't except cheap gifts. Now go and play with yourself general because I am leaving," said Shilpa as she walked towards the door, which she found was locked. "Open it or I will scream in five seconds. Open it now!"

"You think anyone in Tonga is going to come running. They will think you are enjoying yourself. I am a general in the army and you are my woman from today until I get fed up with you, understand? I am a hunter and my aim is good you know."

"Well I am a tigress and so an endangered species. When I sense danger I kill."

The general unzipped his pants and stood there with his 'willy' semi erect.

"Did you forget to take your Viagra general?" Asked Shilpa.

"Shut up this never happens before. I have erection for more than four hours. I am hot, horny man. You take clothes off and see what happens."

"Tell you what next time you have a hard on for four hours give me a call. Till then so-long little hunter," said Shilpa laughing and banged on the door, which opened at once and the guard's jaw dropped seeing the general with his pants down and his 'willy' hanging out.

"Shut the door!" yelled the general as Shilpa breezed out with a big smile on her face. She was never to hear from the general again but the whole of Tonga was to hear her story.

She had decided to stay in one of Tonga's best hotels by the sea where she was treated like royalty and given all the services a princess would receive. Days went into weeks and then months. She occasionally spoke to Oly but no one else in the outside world. He had arranged for $10,000 dollars to be placed in her account every month from her father's account, which amounted to over $7,000,000.

Tonga has two seasons, hot and wet. It was now wet in 2011 but the rain was warm so Shilpa decided to put on a sarong and a tee-shirt she had bought from India that said *Mumbai- the Manhattan of India*. They must be bloody joking she thought while putting it on. The reason she liked it was because it was a gift from her maid.

The rains bring with them spectacular sunsets, all the colours of the prism, which can be seen on the long, white sand beaches where Shilpa decided to stroll. There were a few tourists playing on the sands and a couple of kids in the ocean, she stopped to watch them play and then heard, "Peter, Jill come out of the sea is too rough now," shouted a mother. Peter came out and ran towards her but Jill still kept jumping over the waves. "Jill get back now do you hear me or you are grounded tomorrow, Jill!"

Shilpa knees gave way and she sank under a palm tree. Jill, my Jill, my love what have I done? She stared out at the ocean and she found herself touching Jill's body, kissing her beautiful feet with pink nail varnish, caressing her breasts and kissing those voluptuous lips. She was with her naked on the bed in Bombay, playing with her hair in Green Park, then astride her that last night. Oh my God what have I done to myself?

"Can I help you madam?" Said the beach boy who looked after the chairs.

Shilpa looked up and stared at him. Her face was covered in sand from her palms, which were full of the white sand that had her lips imprints in them. The tears ran down her face creating canals through the sand that caked that stunning countenance.

The boy looked doleful when he saw that she had been crying and offered to bring some water from the bar and wash her face. He poured the water from the jug gently on the forehead and then over her cheeks to wash away the sand. Shilpa dropped her hands and let the water cascade over her cheeks till they were clean but the tears still kept rolling down.

"Madam please let me help you to your room," said the boy. Shilpa without a word took his arm and walked to her room. She decided to take a pill to sleep something she hadn't done in months.

As she slept a call came to the room from reception. "Madam a good friend wants to see you can he come up please? He says it's a surprise."

"Who is it? Man or woman?"

"Man mam he is not willing to give his name but he says you will be happy to see him," said the receptionist.

"OK tell Oly to come up," said Shilpa.

She left the door open and went to pour a couple of glasses of lemonade for the two of them.

"Hello Shilpa," said the man at the door.

Shilpa whipped around and stared for full five seconds and her heart rate went from 90 to 140.

"Where the hell did you come from? Jesus Christ! How the hell did you find me?" cried Shilpa.

"We have our ways and means don't we in the office," said Tito.

"I know enough people here to get you killed you know," said Shilpa.

"Well not before I kill you my darling. I am under orders. You killed one of ours and that is unforgiveable, you know that," said Tito very calmly. "It's over Shilpa."

Tito drew his gun from the back of his trousers and fired. Shilpa screamed and then her jaw dropped. At the end of the barrel was the Union Jack. He began to laugh as Shilpa walked up to him and slapped him on the face over and over again. He just stood there and took it.

"What would you say if I asked you to marry me?" he said.

"Nothing, I can't talk and laugh at the same time you dumb ox."

Tito looked around the room and walked to the bar and drank from the glass of lemonade. "Tell me what's it like to fall into heaven," asked Tito

"You tell me what's it like to be kicked out of hell. How did you find me in the first place?"

"You may think I am a dumb ox but I followed the money. It wasn't easy but I traced you to Zurich and met that countryman of mine Olivetti. Interesting man, leads a double life. Keeps you in Zurich as a bachelor and three kids and an older wife in Roma who he sees once a year. I told him I was MI6-showed my card. Then I told him if he didn't give me the real address of one Shilpa Moray his son's head would be in his bed in three days' time and if he thought I was joking then try me. He didn't, in ten minutes I had everything on you except your bank account he wouldn't give me that. So here I am my Shilpa ready to be of service to you for the rest of your life."

Her father always liked Tito and thought she should marry him so she put her right hand in the top of his trousers and pulled him towards her, they kissed and made love for the rest of the afternoon.

The phone rang "Hello madam was you pleased to see the surprised gentleman? Hope he is not of nuisance to you?" Asked the receptionist.

"No he is fine. We are both fine thank you." Shilpa replaced the receiver but Tito picked it up and asked for room service, turning to Shilpa he asked "How do you like your eggs in morning baby?"

"Unfertilized thank you," she turned over and slept on his chest for the next 8 hours.

When she woke up in the early dawn Tito was staring at her. "You know Tito I have wanted to say these lines for a long time. They are from my two favourite films-"*Casablanca*" and "*Gone with the Wind*"- this time I really mean it. *Tito, this could be the start of a beautiful friendship. After all tomorrow is another day!*"

THE END

AUTHOR

Cyrus Bharucha was born in Bombay but grew up in the UK where he went to Kent College in Canterbury. He started life as a photographer and then joined the BBC where he became a film cameraman and producer for Current Affairs both posts took him around the world and he experienced filming in all genres.

He left BBC TV to go to the USA where he was Executive Producer for PBS producing over 60 programmes; some of his shows like from China to US won major awards and he also worked as a freelance producer-director, his film "Nobody Listens" was nominated for Best Children's drama for the New York Film Festival. "Fireworks-with George Plimpton" got him an ACE-Emmy nomination for best feature documentary. He has travelled around the world, extensively in the Middle East and in Pakistan covering stories for American TV and BBC. He was a founder member of CNN. CEO of TV Asia and worked on the tour of Abel Gance's "Napoleon" for Francis Ford Coppola's Zoetrope amongst other ventures.

Cyrus has also worked in India producing and directing his epic film "On Wings Of Fire" with an international star cast. He has also made several corporate and advertising films in India. He recently made a documentary on the great Indian advocate Nani. A Palkhivala- "Nani- the crusader." He now teaches in several colleges and coaches corporate staff in soft skills.

This is his second novel and a sequel to the first-*Bollywood, Beds & Beyond*.